Cliffhanger

(The Belinda & Bennett Mysteries, Book 1)

Amy Saunders

Cliffhanger

Copyright © 2012 by Amy Saunders

All rights reserved. No part of this book may be reproduced or transmitted in any form or by any means without written permission of the author.

Acknowledgments

I have to thank my ever-patient beta readers for bearing with me through multiple drafts. If it weren't for their honesty and support, I would never have made it this far as a novelist!

Other Titles by Amy Saunders

Biohazard
The Jester's Apprentice
Dead Locked

Table of Contents

Chapter 1 1

Chapter 2 10

Chapter 3 18

Chapter 4 25

Chapter 5 37

Chapter 6 43

Chapter 7 50

Chapter 8 62

Chapter 9 70

Chapter 10 84

Chapter 11 93

Chapter 12 103

Chapter 13 111

Chapter 14 119

Chapter 15 130

Chapter 16 142

Chapter 17 150

Chapter 18 160

Chapter 19	170
Chapter 20	177
Chapter 21	187
Chapter 22	193
Chapter 23	200
Chapter 24	207
Chapter 25	213

Chapter 1

Belinda could have turned left to go directly to the house, but she charged straight through the four-way stop. At the top of the road, before it dipped down and curved inland again, she could just make out the ocean between the blades of wheat-like sea grasses bowing toward her. Pure joy swelled in her chest and she pressed down on the accelerator.

Belinda skidded into the beach parking lot and flung open the door, her face hit by the sea breeze still clinging to winter. She jogged toward the water's edge, jumping around on one bare foot, giggling as she nearly collapsed onto the sand wrenching her other shoe off. My, how that white, gravelly stuff was tougher to walk through than she remembered!

Belinda stopped at the water's edge, the sand itself sending chills up her legs. But she had to do it. She had to dip her feet in the water just once. She secured her blonde hair in an elastic, taking a deep breath of salt air—and, ooh yeah, seaweed. Yuck. Belinda stood on the water mark and waited for the next surge. She closed her eyes as it rushed toward her, bunching up and suppressing a squeal as the Atlantic said hello.

"Hello!" she said back with her arms opened wide, but she dashed back to the safe zone before it could reply.

Shivering and wet and sand covered, Belinda leaned against the craggy rocks creating a natural barrier between the town beach and the rest of it. Belinda gazed out at the horizon, the silhouette of a sailboat moving along it. It had been too long since Kyle sailed. He always shot her down when she suggested it, but she would do her yearly thing and say something anyway. Her feet dried and Belinda finally trudged back to her car, brushing sand off of her feet in the parking lot. Kyle was supposed to leave work early to meet her, so it was time to go home.

She backtracked, cruising along until a familiar house peeked out from a gap in the conical topiary fence. Belinda slowed down, rounding the corner of the driveway, and passed through the open gate and down the brick drive. She parked next to her brother's Jeep and dashed into the house.

"Kyle!" Belinda's voice echoed in the foyer and she headed straight for the open glass door across the hall. She found him lazing in a wood lounger on the back deck with a beer, alt rock blaring out of his earbuds. "Kyle!" Belinda stepped around his legs, arching her eyebrows and waving.

Kyle jumped, ripping the buds out. "Hey, you're early." When his brown eyes lit up, she was practically looking into her own. The one clear sign of their twin-ness from her perspective.

"Actually, I'm late. I detoured to the beach for a minute." Belinda grinned and they bear hugged after he stood up. "Is there anything to eat?" Kyle just offered a lopsided grin. "I'll take that as a no."

"I would have stocked up, but I figured—"

"You figured you would just wait and let me do it."

"No, I was going to say I figured you'd want to get your own stuff."

"And?"

"And that you would get some other things while you were there."

Belinda put her hands on her hips. "Am I going to regret living with you?"

"Probably." Kyle grabbed her shoulders and spun her around. "But look at that view, eh?"

Belinda meandered off the low-lying porch and toward the edge of the property where it dropped off into the sea. It was more protected than other parts of Portside where the houses were right on the open ocean. But the wind and the currents below still tasted wild. Kyle was right. Putting up with him again was worth that view everyday.

"All right," she said, turning around, "I can do this. But you will help me with the housework, or I'm going to tell Mom that you killed her tomatoes and we'll see just how fast they get back from Europe."

"Total accident."

"You ran over them with your dirt bike."

"Accident."

"Dirt bike. In the yard, destroying their finely tuned grass and tomato plants."

Kyle hugged his chest. "They are not going to come back from Europe early for that."

"No, but they might do something drastic like kick you out."

"Hey, if I go, so do you." He pointed at her nose. "I have some pretty sick stories I could tell them about you too."

"From when? High school? Ancient history."

"New York. Art gallery. Not so ancient."

Belinda rolled her eyes to the blue sky, squinting in the light. "Fine. I will forget about the tomato 'accident.' For now." Kyle grinned. "But don't get comfortable. I was an adult for the whole New York thing."

"And I was an adult for the whole running over the tomato plants thing."

Belinda looked back out at the water. Kyle picked up on what was coming next and rolled his eyes. "Bels, don't—"

"It's great weather for sailing today. In fact, I saw someone out on their boat at the beach."

Kyle sighed.

"What?"

"You know what. I don't want to. Not anymore."

Belinda's eyes grew sad. "Mark would hate that you've given it up. He would absolutely hate it."

"Well, he's not here to care, is he?"

Belinda pursed her lips. From the flare of gold in his eyes, that was all she should say on that subject right then. "So what do we do for dinner then?"

Kyle loosened up. "We could crash Victoria's."

"We are not crashing Victoria's." Belinda thought about the other options and scrunched her nose. "Well, maybe this once. I'll call and see if she minds a couple of extra diners."

"I'm used to you being home already."

Belinda wrinkled her nose, working up a retort, when someone called her from the front of the house. She turned to see a young man waving from the entrance. "Oh, no," she mumbled.

Kyle grinned as a tall kid with bright blue eyes smiled broadly and came out to the backyard. "Belinda," he said cheerfully, "you're home! I'd heard talk but...you're actually here." His face beamed.

"Hi, Jarrett." Belinda shifted awkwardly. She gripped Kyle's shirt as he started to walk away, but he pulled free, making smoochy faces at her behind Jarrett's back. Once Kyle was out of earshot, Jarrett stuffed his hands into his pockets and moved in closer. Belinda took a step back, glancing behind her to be sure of the cliff.

"I'm eighteen now," he said.

Belinda blinked. "Oh, well, congratulations. Eighteen...it's a good year." For some people, she imagined.

Jarrett laughed nervously, pulling on his earlobe. "You said to, you know, try again when I was eighteen. So here I am."

Belinda's mouth fell open, but no sound came out.

"You wanna go get a coffee or something?"

Oh, dear, Belinda thought. Really? She just got into Portside and it was already looking like time to leave. "I just got—"

"It doesn't have to be right now. Tomorrow, when you're settled in and all."

"It's not that. I...I'm here to work. I'm overseeing our house renovation and I've got other plans—"

"You're busy; I get it. But coffee, Belinda? I know you like coffee." He flashed a smile, his blue eyes sparkling. She had to admit he was cute, and if she were his age or vice versa, well, maybe.

Belinda shook her head. "Of course I do, but Jarrett—"

"What?" His eyes narrowed ever so slightly.

Belinda wanted to just run into the house and lock the doors. Why wouldn't he just move on already? "Maybe when you're twenty-one."

"Last time you said when I was eighteen."

"Well, twenty-one is the new eighteen."

"Belinda—"

"Jarrett, we've been over this. Several times. And my opinion that you are too young for me has not changed." Belinda hooked her thumbs in her back pockets, trying to figure out how to end the conversation. "There are lots of girls your age." There. That should pacify him.

"They're all silly."

Or not. And he was starting to whine.

"They're not all silly. You just need to keep a wary eye open. Besides, you're headed off to college. You'll meet more girls there."

"I wouldn't have to if you would just go out with me."

Belinda sighed, not mentally prepared for a debate.

"We get along." Jarrett put his hands out toward her pleadingly. "We have great conversations. I don't see what the problem is."

"I know you don't, but please try and see this from my perspective. You're a smart guy, you can surely imagine."

Jarrett didn't look to Belinda like he was trying that hard, but his sour face slowly reverted back to a smile. "I don't have that great of an imagination."

Belinda crossed her arms. "I beg to differ."

"Anyway," Jarrett inched closer, "my band is practicing this Saturday afternoon. You should come. You like alt rock, right?"

How did he do that? After that whole conversation, he just glossed over it like nothing happened. No matter how mean she acted, he kept coming back for more.

"We're not that bad either. We've been practicing really hard. Even played at a few parties." Jarrett rocked on his heels.

"That's terrific, Jarrett. But I..." Why did he refuse to be reasonable? And why did she have such a hard time telling him to get lost? "I'll see." Belinda slumped over.

Jarrett grinned. "You won't be sorry."

Oh, yes, I will, Belinda thought.

Just a few streets away stood Victoria's and Dan's pomegranate-color house or the Pom-Pom house as they'd nicknamed it when they moved in a few years ago. Belinda was always surprised by how shady it was there, but they actually had trees in their yard. Waiting with the door open was a five-foot-three, copper-haired woman in a floral skirt. She and Belinda bounced up and down at the sight of each other. When the complimenting and talking all at once finished, they took to the bench off of the kitchen.

"We're so glad you're back!" Victoria said, squeezing Belinda's hands from across the table.

"Well, who else is going to see that the house renovation goes smoothly while my parents are gone?"

"Kyle?"

Belinda laughed, poking Kyle as he snarled. "I could handle this...if I wanted to."

Belinda rolled her eyes. "Well, Mom and Dad asking me to come back to do this works out anyway." Her whole countenance brightened. "I have a cupcake boutique to get off the ground, and you and I have scouting to do."

Victoria grinned. "Are we about to repeat the great beach cookout catastrophe?"

"Ugh." Belinda ran her tongue across her teeth. "I still have sand in my mouth from that."

"My mom had to throw out some of her cookware, you know. My dad insisted he had grit in his food whenever she'd use them."

"Those were the days. When we made off with your mom's world-class cookware to use on the beach of all places." They both laughed. "Neither of us knew much back then."

"Now I think we know too much." Victoria frowned. "Dan sends his love, but he had to eat already and get back to work. He's at the end of a big job right now." She rested her chin on the heel of her palm. "I can't wait until it's finished."

"Will he be joining you for the reunion?" Belinda said, dishing out some of Victoria's homemade mac-n-cheese.

"Thankfully, yes. Since neither of you is going, I'm going to need him for moral support."

"You could hardly count Kyle as moral support anyway," Belinda said.

"Hey! I resent that."

"Well, it's true. I love you and all that, but most of the time you were off flirting in high school and I can't imagine our tenth reunion would be much different."

Victoria glanced between them. "Do I have any takers for the after-reunion party at the Mayhew house?"

Kyle snorted.

Belinda twirled her fork.

"You're not even considering it, right?" Kyle said.

Belinda smiled sheepishly. "If he's not in town..."

Kyle arched his eyebrows, rubbing the bone right above one of them. "You'll regret it. Even if he isn't here, you'll regret going." Kyle popped a piece of roll into his mouth as he spoke. "You've already been accosted by one jilted lover. Do you really want to try for two?"

Victoria glanced between the two of them. "What other jilted lover are we discussing?"

"Jarrett paid her a visit," Kyle said gleefully.

"Already?" Victoria arched her eyebrows.

"He only lives next door," Belinda said nonchalantly. "He saw me drive in."

"Wow." Victoria sat back. "You make one whale of an impression at pool parties."

"I had no idea that innocently popping into something I was invited to would get this intense."

"The kid has guts."

"Yep. A sixteen-year-old walks right up to me at his pool party and asks me out without the slightest concern that I might say no, but I can't find someone of legal age with the same tenacity."

Kyle cleared his throat. "Um, excuse me, but Jarrett is eighteen now."

Belinda's head whipped around. "I thought you left before he said that."

"I kept in hearing distance."

Belinda sighed. "Is Jeff in town for the reunion?"

"To my knowledge, no," Victoria said.

"But none of us are besties with these people anymore," Kyle said. "He could be here and none of us know about it. It's not a stretch."

Belinda nodded. She knew that. She did. But the thought that Jeff wouldn't be around and it might be safe to go tempted her.

Kyle sighed, digging his fingers into his short-cropped brown hair. "Do I have to forbid you to go? Because I will."

Belinda narrowed her eyes, daring him to say it.

After a ten-second stare down he crumpled. "You get on me for things constantly," he mumbled.

"Don't worry," Victoria said. "I'll look after her."

That conversation knotted up Kyle's good mood and he turned all frowny faced for the rest of the night. Belinda knew how sensitive he was to that topic, and she hated trying to bring it up around him. But she felt confident that the reunion after-party, as Victoria had called it, would be fine. And if it wasn't, she wasn't obligated to stay. Belinda would just turn around and zip back home. Done and done. She left Kyle to his video games and went to unpack and find an appropriate outfit for the party.

Chapter 2

Bennett Tate adjusted the final camera in the Mayhew house hallway and climbed down the stepladder. Private party jobs were both simple and tricky. Simple because there usually wasn't as much space to cover and his clients generally asked for basic security. Tricky because they also wanted everything incredibly low-profile, which was easier said than done. But Bennett had managed to develop an event security firm known for its transparency and discretion at these sorts of events. He'd done it before, he could do it again.

He jogged to the room down the hallway that served as his headquarters, his anticipation building as it got closer to party time. His associate, Finnegan, manned the desk at that moment, checking all the cameras to make sure everything worked. They still had plenty of time before guests were set to arrive, but Bennett liked to be ahead of the game. He crossed behind Finnegan's seat, leaning over to see that they had visuals on all sides.

"Everything's ready," Finnegan said, chomping on a piece of gum.

"Is that what you're wearing?"

Finnegan checked out his black windbreaker. "What's wrong with it?"

"Nothing. I just want you to blend in. As far as the guests are concerned, we're not supposed to exist."

Finnegan frowned. "What about Rachel?"

"She's blending in too. This is a quick job. Shouldn't be much trouble with this crowd."

"Except that the client's paranoid someone will steal from him."

"Look at this place." Bennett demonstrated by glancing at the room. "Do you blame him?"

"No. But it's an odd setup to have your friends over."

From the size of the guest list, Bennett doubted his client knew any of them that well. It looked like more of an opportunity to show off. "We're just here to do a job, so quit worrying about it."

Finnegan flicked the top of his ear. "Am I on the outside again?"

"Just like we talked about. You can casually walk around once or twice if you want to, but be cool about it. We don't want to arouse suspicion."

"Wouldn't dream of it." Finnegan twirled his thumbs. "Maybe I'll nab a hot date from this."

Bennett set a firm hand on Finnegan's shoulder. "No harassing the guests. You've already annoyed one client in that department."

"I wasn't harassing her guests."

"No, you were harassing her."

Finnegan smirked. "She would've been worth it."

"Yeah, except she already had a boyfriend with more money and muscles than you." He liked Finnegan. Most of the time. But he could be incredibly ridiculous. "You're fortunate she found it amusing and kept it to herself." And they were fortunate that she wasn't that influential in the community.

Finnegan swiveled around in his chair. "At least I try. You bring in someone hot like Rachel for a job and you just completely ignore her." He leaned forward. "She's totally been flirting with you, man. If she flirted with me..."

Bennett's gray eyes tightened. "You know what, go home and change. You're not dressed appropriately."

"Change into what?"

ess casual. Hurry up. Guests should be arriving in
Finnegan slumped out the door, his thin shoulders
blazer!"

:ked at the tip of his chin, staring blankly at the laptop computer screen, displaying empty hallways, except for the occasional caterer. By the time Finnegan returned in slightly better apparel, guests had trickled into the living room, cleared of furniture to serve as a dance floor. That should be interesting, Bennett thought, examining the few people who had showed up so far. If nothing else, maybe the job would be entertaining.

~ * ~

Belinda felt the music reverberate across the stone driveway before she actually heard it. Apparently, Stellan Mayhew still knew how to party. She dropped her keys in the valet's palm, trying to stop herself from mussing her updo, smoothing down the hem of her silk halter top to give her hands something to do. Belinda took one last deep breath of salt air as a woman wearing feather earrings checked her name off a digital list and swung open the door for her.

She stepped into what she remembered being the Mayhew house living room, which was really just a showpiece. She never remembered actually sitting there. The room was unrecognizable as a DJ played the latest dance music from his laptop and pink and blue lights followed the thrashing bodies around the open floor. Most of her former classmates clung to the side walls, relaxed against the mantle, or hung over the second-story railing to watch. Belinda examined her options and not seeing anyone she recognized immediately downstairs, she went up.

Cliffhanger

Belinda heard a squeal before she reached the top. How did anyone have the lung capacity to overcome the *thump, thump, thump* of the bass line? Victoria shuffled over on her tiptoes, practically on her toe nails from the height of her heels. Belinda still had to hunch over a little to give her a hug. Before she'd said hello, Victoria gripped her wrists and led her into a hallway, past what looked like a security guard, and onto a balcony looking out over the ocean.

"I like our little piece of property," Victoria said, the moonlight highlighting her splash of orange hair, "but this is still the best location in Portside." She took Belinda's hand again. "So Kyle didn't come with you."

Belinda shrugged, butterflies swarming in her stomach. "Things will never be the same for him."

"We'll never be the same for him."

"Not you. He still loves you and Dan. It's just...the accident kind of took all the fun out of this place."

"I'm shocked he came back."

Belinda pulled hair out of her mouth, her coif slowly falling apart at the seams with the breeze. "Well, living in our old home sure beats what we'd have on our own. And our parents would rather we live there than leave it empty whilst they travel the world." Victoria leaned back on the railing and pooched out her stomach. Belinda crooked an eyebrow. "Are you trying to tell me something?"

Victoria gazed coyly at the moon. "Maybe."

"Do I detect the beginnings of a bump?" Victoria nodded emphatically. "Too much ice cream?" Victoria swatted her shoulder with her clutch. Belinda laughed. "Too much something apparently. How's Dan?"

"Content as usual." Victoria flicked her head.

Belinda smiled, giving her friend a bear hug. "I better do this before you blow up."

"Dan has been hugging me every five seconds. Says he's trying to fill up before he can't put his arms around me."

"Nice."

"Isn't he though?"

Belinda looked down to the lawn, a man hurrying toward the gazebo, built up to look over the water, with a woman trying to catch up. Belinda glanced at Victoria who was also watching them intently. Once they were inside the structure, the woman flailed her arms about, the words "long time ago" drifting on the air. Victoria cleared her throat and motioned her head toward the hallway, quietly returning there. Belinda gazed out at the couple, but followed Victoria's example. She nodded at the guard as they passed and they made their way back downstairs.

"I'll find Dan," Victoria said, louder now. "He'll want to say hi."

Belinda nodded and pointed to the hallway, attempting to make a sign for bathroom. Victoria put two thumbs up and Belinda left her to find her husband, which should not have been hard knowing Dan. He was either hiding outside or in one of the back rooms.

Belinda peeked down the hallway, grateful to escape the pulse of the living room, and tried not to get her heels caught on the carpet. She kept her hand on the beige wall, scanning her memory for where the bathroom was and turned knobs as she wandered, most of them locked. She probably would have given up the hunt at that point, except for the hushed voices coming from a nearby room. She clung to the wall, quietly inching toward the door, her pulse racing. One of the men was definitely Jeff. Victoria had been positive that Jeff was still on the other side of the country. After all that time, Belinda supposed it no longer mattered. On the other hand, Jeff had a way of clinging to the past.

"We stick to our original plan," Stellan said firmly. "You've held out this long, you can keep going."

"I don't know if I can do that anymore." Jeff sounded tired, but not in a physical sense.

"It's been years; it's fine."

"How is this fine?" Jeff's voice reached a level so she didn't have to strain to hear anymore. Stellan shushed him. "Nothing's been fine since then. Nothing. I've tried to forget but I can't, Stell. I can't forget anything from that day."

Belinda's ears tuned in even more. That day. The day of the sailing accident?

"Keep your voice down," Stellan said sharply.

Jeff made no response.

"You're not to say a word, Jeff. Do you hear me? Not a word."

The hair on Belinda's back sprung up as Stellan hissed the last sentence.

~ * ~

Bennett watched the young woman jiggle knob after knob, wandering through the maze of rooms. Now she just paused as if in concentration. Either that or she was drunk and confused. Or a thief pondering her next move. She was the worst thief in Portside if that was the case. He swiveled back and forth in his seat with his fingers laced over his stomach, watching the laptop screens. She was the only person wandering the hallways. All the other party-goers were actually at the party.

So far this was the least exciting event he'd worked in ages. He was actually relieved when the rogue guest came into view in the hallway. He zoomed in on her so instead of taking up the bottom corner of the screen, she filled it. She still stood motionless, other than swaying a little on her feet. She could be lost. Or his camera could be stuck. He could get Finnegan over there to check things out, but he was just down the hall and could easily do it himself.

Bennett sprung up, happy to have an excuse to move and quietly exited the room. He'd made a point to keep the room dark to avoid suspicion and stayed quiet as possible while monitoring things. He padded in the direction of the lost woman with his hands dug in his denim pockets. He found her around the corner in the same spot. At least now he knew his camera worked. He paused behind her, but she didn't notice. He could hear chatter somewhere nearby though. An eavesdropper?

Bennett casually brushed by her, grazing her bare shoulder with his blazer. She jumped, started to screw up her nose in irritation, then seemed to think better of it and smiled. Bennett crooked up one corner of his mouth slightly in response, taking stock of her. She didn't look like a career woman or a party girl. And she looked worried. Her eyes searched his face, probably trying to place him. In the end, they were full of question marks.

"Do you know where the bathroom is?" she whispered.

Yep. Eavesdropper.

He pointed in the opposite direction, then walked that way, glancing back as a cue to follow him. She hesitated, but he wasn't giving her a way out so she followed, taking about four steps for every one of his. They came to the bathroom door and stopped. She looked at Bennett, then at the door, then back to him, drumming her fingers on her bag. Finally, she switched hands, sticking out the right one toward him. "I'm Belinda Kittridge."

Volunteering her name for the records. Excellent.

"I honestly don't recognize you," she said. "Are you a friend of Stellan's?" Bennett shook her hand, mostly because she wasn't putting it down.

"No," he said, and ignoring her shocked face, walked by her and down the hall just enough to fade into the shadows but still close enough to see what she did once he left.

She squinted to make him out in the dark, putting her hands on her hips and jutting her chin out. Belinda stayed in that position for a few seconds, clearly hurling curse words in his general direction. Bennett licked his lips and waited. Sure enough, once she felt safe that he was out of sight, she drifted back in the direction of the behind-closed-doors conversation. He marched back in her direction, making enough noise so she would hear, and then hid. Fawn Eyes scuttled back to the bathroom door, knocked faintly, and disappeared inside.

Bennett chuckled to himself and meandered back to his post at the monitors, briefly checking in with Finnegan. He yawned, resting his head on his palms, unintentionally keeping his eye on the camera nearest the bathroom. Fawn Eyes finally emerged, peeked around her, and walked straight ahead. He leaned forward again, waiting for her to reappear. She did and stiffened when a man entered the picture. Bennett cocked his head. He'd seen that guy on the monitors earlier...with a woman he thought. They must have gone outside and reentered a different way because he never saw either of them again.

Fawn Eyes shifted her weight several times in the interchange and took micro steps backward. But the man wasn't giving her an out and kept following her with every retreating step. Bennett flipped his phone around and around on the table, debating if he should give Finnegan a call to do a casual walk-by and give Belinda Kittridge an escape. As he was about to, Bennett's client appeared on screen, slapped the other man's back, then shook her hand. After a minute, his client seemed to give her an escape route, which she took in a hurry. His client kept an arm around his friend, leading him out of the camera's eye.

Chapter 3

Belinda speed-walked back toward the obnoxious music, which now made her head hurt. She ignored everyone she passed, searching for Victoria to say good-bye and then she was out of there. Victoria's red head finally appeared out of the crowd. She was leaning to one side, chatting with an unexpected guest. Belinda's stomach twisted. Out of one awkward situation and into an even worse one. Good thing she skipped the reunion.

Lily Devore's dark eyes lit up with as much confusion as her own, but then immediately turned to disdain as she looked Belinda over. "Belinda." She said it like her name left a bad aftertaste. "I didn't expect to find you here."

Belinda folded her arms. "Likewise."

"Back for the reunion?"

"No. You?"

Lily hesitated. "No."

"Here long?" Belinda seriously hoped she said no.

"Just a short visit. You?" Lily raised one of her black eyebrows, her intense blue eye shadow shimmering under the lights passing over them.

Belinda wanted nothing more than to be rid of this pointless exchange. "Undecided."

Victoria glanced from Belinda to Lily and back. Then dead silence, unless you counted the bass shooting up through her toes.

"Are you okay?" Victoria said, touching Belinda's arm. Her cheeks were flushed crimson.

Belinda ran through the scenario in her mind and decided it was better to hold off telling her about it. She wasn't getting into that with Lily Devore present. "I'll tell you later."

Victoria nodded in understanding. She could very well guess what happened anyway. She knew Belinda well enough.

Belinda hugged her good-bye, in case she was huge before they saw each other again, and after exchanging glowers with Lily, she fast-tracked it to the nearest exit, which happened to be a French door leading out into the yard. Her heels sunk into the dirt and she dug through her purse for the valet stub.

Lost in thought, Belinda was vaguely aware in that sixth-sense sort of way that someone else was present in the yard behind her, but she wasn't fast enough to avoid the hand that clutched her arm. "Jeff!" Belinda landed unsteadily on one foot as her heel sunk into the turf. "You scared me!" She could feel her legs taking her backwards. Without giving a signal, they knew she wanted out.

"Ssh!" Jeff glanced back at the house, his eyes darting around. Belinda couldn't see their color in the darkness, but she knew they were sometimes blue, sometimes gray depending on what he wore. "I need to talk to you about something. It's important. Can I come see you tomorrow afternoon?"

Belinda's gut reaction was to find Kyle. But Kyle was home. "I—"

"I promise it has nothing to do with all of that."

Belinda tried to discern if Jeff was drunk. Though his eyes were frantic, they were also clear.

"I trust you," he said. "And I need someone I can trust."

Belinda wished she could feel as certain about him.

Pieces of brown hair flopped at different angles around Jeff's face. His hair wasn't exactly long—on purpose anyway—but long like he needed a cut. "I know you don't want to see me, and I'm sorry for all I put you and your family through. I don't expect you not to hate me, but I do trust you. More than anyone I think."

"That's an intense statement considering I haven't seen you in years." Belinda's fear was starting to be replaced by pity.

"Please, Belinda. I have to tell someone. I can't live like this anymore."

Belinda's heart throbbed. All Jeff had put her through...but look at him now. Look at what life had done to him. "What's bothering you?"

Jeff swallowed. "It's about Mark." He lowered his voice so she almost couldn't hear him.

Belinda's eyes went wide. "About the accident?" Belinda mimicked his voice level.

He nodded emphatically, urgency rippling through his face.

Belinda knew what Kyle would say but her gut told her to say yes. She nodded in consent. "Let's talk then."

Jeff relaxed and the squall in his eyes calmed down. "Thank you, Belinda. Thank you so much." He went to reach for her, but stopped himself as she tensed up.

Jeff half-smiled instead and after looking around him like a spy in trouble, he skittered back toward the side of the house. Belinda turned to go, catching sight of Lily's dark eyes watching her through the glass doors. Lily looked away quickly when Belinda made eye contact. Belinda fled before anyone else accosted her.

She zoomed along the narrow curves and stone walls of Ocean Avenue in her Mini Cooper, darting across town back to her house. She calmed down almost the second she pulled into the driveway. The microwave beeped when she entered the kitchen, the smell of fake butter sitting in the air. Belinda crashed into one of the island stools, resting her still hot cheeks on the cool granite. Kyle ripped open the popcorn bag, shaking it in her direction. "Want some?" he said with his mouth full.

"Sure."

"The box is in the cabinet."

Belinda lifted her head enough to throw the plastic spoon next to her at his face. She missed.

Kyle grinned, shoving another handful into his mouth. "I'm kidding, I'm kidding." He pulled out the box and slid it in her direction. Belinda held her awkward position to keep glaring. "Still kidding." He held up his hands in surrender, ripped open the plastic bag and tossed the popcorn in the microwave. "Rough party, I take it."

She felt safe to relax and went back to pressing her forehead on the counter, images of Jeff flashing in her mind. And Lily. Ugh. "You have no idea." Kyle could have an idea if she just told him who she bumped into, but she'd already dealt with his bad mood the night before and didn't want to go there again so soon.

Kyle munched on the popcorn, licking his fingers. "If you're going to keep living here, you may need to scare up a new set of friends."

"They're not really my friends. Well, except Victoria and Dan." Belinda lifted her head. "I haven't seen or spoken to the rest of them in forever."

"And tonight no doubt assured you of why that is."

"I can't answer that. I talked to like two people."

"But that was enough."

Belinda toyed with an earring. "Maybe."

Kyle laughed. "Bels, it's like eight o'clock."

"It's nine."

"Fine, nine o'clock. Should you be home by nine o'clock? I don't think so. You hated it."

Belinda grinned. "I'm old. Too old for late night partying."

"Then you're old and you hated it." Belinda threw an escaped popcorn kernel at his face. It was barely spring and his skin already glowed. That the boy in the family had been sun kissed instead of her was a complete genetic miscalculation in her books. Kyle smiled. The boyish, aren't-I-adorable-so-you-have-to-let-it-slide smile he always pulled out when he'd been naughty. She swore he had a compartment of smiles in his brain, one for every occasion. Belinda had seen this one more than she could count. But it still worked.

"For the record, you're older than me," Belinda said.

And he'd won. "Only by a minute."

"That's one minute I'm going to cash in for the rest of our lives." Belinda dumped the popcorn into a bowl. There was something wonderful about fake food when you were upset. "It's good you didn't go. I sensed the presence of a certain stalker."

Kyle screwed up his nose the same way Belinda always did. "Carly the Klepto?" Kyle's voice wavered. "Sh–she's still around?" Carly the Klepto, the only woman who truly scared Kyle.

"I think she is. You better watch it."

"Yet another reason to seek out new friends."

"Oh, I'm sure she's moved on by now."

Kyle shivered. "With a nickname like that, I wouldn't be sure of anything." Belinda grinned happily. "Stop reveling in my natural fear of predatory women and eat your popcorn."

Belinda licked her fingers, in a much better mood than when she first got home. "Have you started packing up your room yet?"

Kyle made a face.

"I got boxes for you and everything. All you have to do is throw your stuff inside of them. It's not difficult."

Kyle made another face. Belinda rolled her eyes and flung an empty cardboard box at him. "Then you can help me pack up some of these pots and pans while you're just standing here."

Kyle sighed and set the box on top of the island while Belinda pulled out pots and handed them to him to stack and box. They weren't going far—just to the carriage house out front while her parents had the house interior ripped apart and redone—so Belinda wasn't too worried about how everything was put together. Except for the plates. The plates and glasses were going to be a scene and a half with the dining room china cabinet. Thinking about the work involved there, Belinda started shoving things at Kyle more quickly. Otherwise she was going to have a panic attack just thinking about it.

"So we have a million other things to do this week to get ready to move—and to make room for the demolition." Belinda handed him a nested stack of frying pans. "Besides packing everything up and moving it, we have to deal with the furniture so it's not demolished with the tile."

"I thought we had a moving company taking it all away to storage for us."

Belinda paused, her hand in motion to pick up another sauce pot, flushed from the party, the moving pressure, and her tense reunion with Jeff Clark. Or more to the point, the mention of Mark and the sailing accident. She'd managed not to give it much thought, but now her mind involuntarily kept switching to images of Mark. She handed the pot to Kyle and leaned against the counter to catch her breath.

"All we have to worry about is this stuff, and you need to be here for the movers." Kyle stuffed a handful of popcorn into his mouth.

"I love you." Belinda slowed her pace. "I totally forgot we had professional help for that."

Kyle snickered. "Maybe they can help you too." Belinda glowered and slammed another pot into his chest. As she did so, she caught sight of a long scratch across his forearm where Kyle's sleeve was pushed up.

"What did you do to your arm?"

Kyle glanced at it automatically. "I think I scraped it on a piece of metal or something. You know how crammed the yard is this time of year."

"Are your shots up to date?"

Kyle blinked. "Am I a dog?"

"You can get some pretty nasty infections from rusted metal, Kyle. I'm just asking."

Kyle shrugged. "It's nothing. I'll slap some disinfectant on it before bed, okay?"

With more of that work out of the way, Belinda crashed in her bedroom, pretty stark with no one inhabiting it on a permanent basis for years. She sat on the edge of the shabby chic comforter and re-read the note card her mom had left on the dresser. Belinda remembered when her parents built the house when they were teens. It was strange and yet comforting coming back to it. Getting all misty-eyed, she set the card so she could see the puppies on the front from bed.

She forced herself to turn off the light, closing her eyes on the thoughts of how best to pack up the plates and arrange everything. As she drifted off, those concerns were replaced by ones from the party. The strange conversation she overheard, obnoxious Lily, and the intensity in Jeff's eyes when he mentioned Mark.

Mark. Now that subject brought up a whole bunch of other feelings that could keep her awake for days. Belinda flopped over on her back and stared into the dark. It was gonna be a long night.

Chapter 4

Belinda's cell phone buzzed and startled her awake much earlier than she cared for after sleeping restlessly. She felt for the phone with her eyes closed, opening one halfway to read the message. She read it once and closed her eye again, then bolted awake, kicking off the covers and running for Kyle's room.

Belinda flew inside and shook him until he finally woke up with a start, eyes crazed, and mumbling something about a fire. She shoved her phone into his face. After over a minute of just staring at it blankly, the words on the screen finally penetrated and his complexion turned from bronze to ash. "Jeff is dead," he croaked.

Belinda cupped her mouth with her hands, now sure she hadn't misunderstood Victoria's text. Kyle met her eyes, disbelief, fear, and something else mixed in his. Torment? Or maybe that was just Belinda's reflection.

Victoria sat with the two of them on their back deck a half-hour later. Stellan Mayhew had contacted Victoria and asked her to pass the information along. A nice gesture, Belinda thought. At least she didn't find out about it from the news. Kyle slurped milk out of a cereal bowl but Belinda had no appetite. She sat curled up in a lounger with her hands wrapped around her stomach.

Before she woke up, Belinda had dreamt about swimming off of Mark's boat. Kyle and two others she couldn't identify disappeared, leaving only gurgling water behind. She guessed they drowned. It was disturbing, but now she felt a new wave of disturbed. Emptiness. Relief. Guilt. Sickness. All of these tried to control her at once. So she emptied herself of feeling and chose numbness.

"So they think he jumped?" she said rather neutrally, though Belinda felt anything but neutral, especially looking out at their view. Their property line ended in a similar plunge toward the water. She gripped her shirt to keep from shaking.

"I guess," Victoria said, staring up at the sky through sunglasses. "I didn't want to bug Stellan with a lot of questions."

"When did it happen?"

"All I know is that it was some time last night."

"I saw him last night. Did I tell you that?"

Victoria turned to see Belinda. "No, you didn't, but I assumed from the way you ran out of there."

"This was after that, on my way to get my car. He wanted to see me."

Kyle snapped to. "You didn't tell me you saw Jeff."

Belinda groaned. "Did I have to? Wasn't my blatant misery and early return enough?"

Kyle shrugged. "I thought you just hated the party in general. What did he say?"

Belinda sighed. "Nothing. Stellan showed up before he could get anything out." She shivered thinking about Jeff's skittish expression at the party like he was being watched. What did he want to tell her about Mark and the accident?

Kyle put his cereal bowl down and stared out at the water, the sun glistening off the ripples. The current was fierce that morning, visible on top of the waves. It would be good sailing weather, circumstances aside. "I'm sorry, Bels. Maybe I shouldn't have encouraged you to come back."

Belinda slowly changed her position, her legs going numb. "I came back of my own volition. I knew I'd see him again eventually."

Cliffhanger

"I think he'd actually gotten worse," Victoria said. "Dan and I talked about it last night and we both felt like something was gnawing at Jeff."

"He never got past Mark's death," Kyle said, gripping the chair arms. "Jeff blamed himself more than Stellan for what happened."

"I've always wondered why," Victoria said. "I know Stellan was affected, but it hit Jeff the hardest. Stellan seemed to shake off the blame."

"Jeff was more sensitive." Belinda returned to her curled up position in the chair. Is that what Jeff wanted to say to her so badly? Did it connect to what Jeff told Stellan?

"Jeff should've stayed in California," Kyle said. "He might have forgotten eventually." Belinda and Victoria exchanged glances. Kyle turned to both of them and pulled out one of his secret weapon smiles. "Bels needs to eat. Let's go make pancakes."

~ * ~

Jonas Parker leaned over the cliff's edge as far as he could and dared, examining the rocks below. He held his tie down to keep it from blowing up in his face, but then his light brown hair blew into his eyes anyway. It was amazing that Jeff Clark's body had not been swept away, and fortunate that a man who worked for the Mayhews spotted it early that morning. Jonas looked down to where the body had been and repressed a shudder. What a way to go.

"Detective!" Bennett sauntered across the lawn toward him.

Jonas jumped, quickly stepping away from his perch and darker thoughts. They shook hands, Jonas slapping Bennett on the shoulder.

"Congrats on the promotion. Way to get broken in." Bennett swung his head in the water's direction. "You asked to see me?"

Jonas rubbed his chin. "I'm hoping you'll have something from the party last night for us to work with."

Bennett nodded, sifting through what he knew had happened. "You don't think he jumped?"

Jonas shrugged. "Too early to say. It's possible. All we have so far is what appears to be a note to someone named Mark in the victim's pocket, an empty beer bottle on the cliff's edge, and traces of some white stuff on the grass. The only person living in the house right now, one of the Mayhew kids, thought the victim had left, but he didn't park with the valet service and his car is not at his grandparents' house, which is where he was staying. I could use your insider information to narrow things down."

"I've got plenty of footage of empty hallways."

Jonas laughed. "What? Nobody snuck off to snog in one of the bedrooms?"

"All the bedrooms were locked. And I think this crew is past their partying prime."

"Aren't we all? Well, I'd like to go over the footage with you first, if you don't mind. You might have some insight on who we're dealing with."

Bennett had brought his equipment for that reason and they set it up in the same room he'd occupied the night before. Lots of empty hallways as promised, some bad dance moves, and a few odd hallway moments. They watched the victim, Jeff, and a woman as yet unidentified, go outside in a hurry. Then there was Belinda.

"Fawn Eyes," Bennett muttered. Jonas raised an eyebrow. Bennett pursed his lips as he came on the screen.

Cliffhanger

Several minutes later, Belinda reappeared in the same spot, talking to the victim and then the client. Jonas marked something down on his phone.

"And that's the extent of the people activity beyond the party," Bennett said. "At least, on camera. You'll want to talk to Finn about what happened outside." Bennett tore his eyes off the monitor and slid a printout of the guest list across the desk. "I only have names this time, no photos. I'm also under the impression that most of these people no longer live in the area but were just in town for their high school reunion."

Jonas arched one brown eyebrow. "Thrilling. No wonder none of them could dance." He pocketed the list. "So, should I start my inquiries with Fawn Eyes?"

Bennett twirled his thumbs, staring at the black and white image of Belinda Kittridge. Real life did her more justice. "It's your call, Detective."

Jonas swiveled around in the office chair, lifting his feet off the ground to do a full circle. "She had an unpleasant meeting with the vic and ran from the party right afterward. So I'd have to say she's first on my obvious list."

"Your 'obvious list'?"

"My list of people who obviously know something about what's going on with my dead guy." Bennett's eyes eagerly wandered back to the screen. "Maybe you should get that shot printed out. It is the best one after all."

Bennett glowered and shut the laptop.

"Why are you so touchy? You know, Finn warned me you were in a mood, but I told him he just doesn't understand you." Jonas grinned.

"This is work, and right now she's a suspect." Bennett started to pack up his equipment.

Jonas took stock of his friend. "You know..."

Bennett wrestled with getting the laptop back in its case. "You know what?" His voice was crisp like he knew what came after that. Maybe now wasn't the right time to finish the thought.

"Never mind. Thanks for the help, bro." Jonas threw his jacket back on.

"Anytime." Bennett was now consumed with his repacking, or more likely with other less pleasant thoughts, so Jonas left him to it and went to interview Belinda Kittridge.

~ * ~

Belinda had finally settled down enough to crack open her laptop to browse wedding registry items for her cousin's upcoming shower when the doorbell rang. Reluctantly, she pushed herself off the couch and opened the door to Jonas Parker. He smiled, a bit lopsided, and explained why he was there. Belinda escorted him to the back porch, thinking it would have a calming effect on her.

"I have to say...wow." He crashed into a lounger, the wind undoing his forward-brushed light brown hair, hurling wisps of it straight up into the air. He didn't seem to take any notice and just absorbed the surroundings for a few minutes. Belinda waited with her hands clasped in her lap, perched on the edge of her seat, not quite as relaxed as she'd hoped.

"So I just have a few questions to ask," the detective said after he seemed to get enough of staring at their property. "Nothing too scary. First, I'd just like to know how you knew Jeff Clark."

"Oh...well, that's easy." Belinda swallowed, her mouth going completely dry. "We went to school together and our families knew each other."

"Were you close?" Belinda started to speak then hesitated. Almost like a good TV interviewer, he jumped in. "Is it more complicated than a yes or no answer?"

Cliffhanger

Belinda nodded, her eyes filling with tears. She hadn't cried once yet, or even felt like it. Now, when she needed to hold it together, she was unraveling. "We weren't on the same page about our relationship."

"I see. Was that the cause of your awkward meeting with him at the party?"

All Belinda could do was nod emphatically.

"Was seeing him upsetting to you last night?"

More emphatic nodding. The detective let her compose herself. She took a deep breath, dabbing at her eyes with a sleeve and sniffed. "He...if I had known he would be there, I would have skipped the party."

"What exactly was your relationship like with Jeff?"

"He liked me, a long time ago, in high school." Belinda fought to remember what had actually happened. Some things stuck out too much and others not enough. "I didn't feel that way about him, but before I got a chance to be clear on that, he suffered a tragedy."

Jonas leaned forward on his knees, his brow creased up in concentration.

"You may remember from the news," she continued, feeling choked up again, "but one of our friends died in a horrible sailing accident about ten years ago." The detective nodded. "Well, Jeff was with him when he drowned. I mean, he was one of the boys on the sailboat when it happened. And...and he was never the same person after that."

"So did he drop his interest in you?"

Belinda shook her head. "The opposite happened. He became somewhat obsessed with it to the point that my family had to leave town for a while. He did calm down, thankfully, but," Belinda thought back to him in Stellan's yard, "he always insisted it didn't work out because of the accident. Because he wasn't the same person after it."

"But that wasn't the case."

"No. It wasn't."

"Is that what he said to you in the hallway?"

"Well...he didn't really get a chance. I avoided him because we always had the same conversation. That we couldn't be together because of his issues related to the sailing accident. I couldn't deal with it anymore." A shock of terror went through her that he'd think she meant she killed him. "I mean, I just avoided him because of it."

The detective seemed to ignore her blunder.

"Something different happened last night though." Belinda edged closer to the detective. She had to get this out before he switched topics. "Jeff asked to meet me today. He said he had something important to tell me about...about the sailing accident."

Jonas' chill expression intensified. "Do you have any idea what he wanted to say?"

"I can only relate it back to something I overheard between Jeff and Stellan. But it's all out of context."

Jonas leaned forward. "Doesn't matter. Tell me." Belinda related every detail about the conversation that she could recall. It wasn't much, but Jonas took notes, and looked her directly in the eye. "Who else was on that boat when the accident occurred?"

Belinda didn't even have to think. "Jeff, Stellan, and Mark."

He took notes on his phone. "Mark?"

"Yes, Mark Nichols." Belinda looked down.

Jonas tapped his stylus on his phone. "We found a note to a Mark in Clark's pocket. Do you think it could be this Mark Nichols?"

Belinda didn't know how to answer that question. "Well, I suppose it could be, but Mark has been dead for almost ten years." Jonas tilted his head, so Belinda went on to explain. "He was the friend that died in the sailing accident."

Jonas nodded. "Did they sail together often?"

"Oh, yes. My brother was in their group a lot too. And sometimes Mark's girlfriend, Lily Devore."

"Is she still in the area?"

"Not permanently. But she was at the party last night."

"Huh." Jonas glanced up from trying to make out his screen in the sunlight. "So your brother wasn't there that day? Of the sailing accident?"

Belinda almost clapped her hand over her mouth. "No." She bit her lip. "Is this a murder investigation?"

"I honestly don't know yet. Why?"

Belinda turned to look out at the property's edge. "Because I'll tell you right here, that Jeff did not kill himself. He acted his share of crazy, and he was definitely freaking out about something, but I know that he would not have asked to see me that night only to jump off a cliff right afterward." Her voice was shaky but convinced.

Jonas nodded and stood, stretching his long legs out. Belinda followed him around the house to the driveway, looking for his car, but Jonas knocked the kickstand of a bike up and peddled off.

Belinda darted back inside and called Kyle's cell. He answered, sounding a bit distracted. "Got a minute?" she said, pacing around the kitchen island. "I just had a big oops moment and I need to tell you."

"Did you take off with someone else's watermelon again?"

Belinda narrowed her eyes. "That happened once about five years ago. Honestly."

"Okay, okay. What was today's 'oops' moment?"

"Not that I'm in the mood to tell you now, but I talked to the police about Jeff."

"So it was a murder."

"He didn't say that, and as far as I could tell he was just sizing up the situation."

"All right, well go on. I'm sure that's not what you're ramping up to tell me."

"I had to tell him about my relationship, or lack thereof, with Jeff, and it kind of came out that you used to sail with all of them."

"Well, I did."

"I also accidentally mentioned that you weren't there when the accident happened."

Kyle paused. "Well, I wasn't," he said flatly.

"I know. It's just...I don't know..."

"Don't worry, Bels. Jeff is dead and we did hang out a lot at one time. I'm sure they'll want to talk to me at some point. It would've come out anyway. It's not a secret."

"What if they ask—?"

"Then I'll answer. Stop worrying about it. I can take care of myself."

Belinda stared at a photo in the kitchen of the two of them on Mark's sailboat before the accident. No matter what approach she took, the subject always remained taboo. "Are you working?"

"Yes."

"Then I'll let you go."

"Bels—"

"Yeah?"

"Antelope sheep."

Belinda smiled. "Pollywog rattlesnake." Belinda hung up, still stuck on the photo. She'd had all these romantic notions of coming home, imagining that life would be just the same as before. But it wasn't, and Jeff's death only magnified that truth. Nothing would ever be the same.

~ * ~

Jonas got on the phone with Bennett immediately as he hugged the curvy beach road heading back to the station. "Two things," he said, peddling over as a car passed. "Fawn Eyes is not our killer."

"If you even need one." Bennett stowed his laptops away in his home office and locked it up. "Last I checked, the reason for his death was undetermined."

"Second," Jonas was not in the mood to argue about technicalities, "you need to cozy up to her. This woman knows these people, their history. And given the right circumstances, will share that wealth of knowledge."

Bennett stared into his empty fridge. "Then turn back around and go ask her yourself."

"I can't. I don't have a legitimate reason to."

"You're investigating a potential homicide. I vaguely recall that counts as a legitimate reason to question people."

"Yes, but you are not a police officer."

Bennett paused, hand frozen over his keys in claw formation.

"Everyone is on guard with the police, but she wouldn't have to be with you. You could just talk and it's not official." Jonas congratulated himself for his brilliant idea.

"And how would we do that?"

"You bump into each other, you say hi, then you say something else, then she replies, then you ask a question, and so on and so forth. You know, it's called conversation."

Bennett rolled his eyes. "I get that, thank you. But when would I bump into her? I've never seen her before in my life."

"It's like a type of car. You never knew it existed until you buy one and all of the sudden everyone you see owns that same car."

"So Belinda Kittridge is a now an automobile."

"No. Belinda Kittridge is a socialite. A socialite who could offer vital information to our cause." Not to mention attractive and single as far as he could tell.

"I wouldn't describe her that way. She associates with these people but I'm not sure she belongs with them."

Jonas laughed. "You've watched that footage of her a lot today, haven't you?"

Bennett turned blood red and glared at his keys. "I can't help you."

"Oh, yes you can. And you will. Investigating is still in your blood, I can smell it. You made a terrific PI so I'm sure you can find a way to casually run into her somewhere. Then you do your little conversation thing and whammo she tells you something invaluable."

"You do realize I know why you're actually doing this?"

Jonas shrugged. "It'll be good for you. And it beats staring at an aerial view of her walking back and forth in a hallway all day."

Bennett gripped his keys. "We'll see."

Jonas hung up, satisfied that he'd done what he set out to do. If Bennett didn't find her patterns and fall into step with them within two days, Jonas would take an early retirement and go flip hamburgers for the rest of his life.

Bennett returned home about an hour later with his lunch. He sat out in his yard in the shade, perfectly content to sit there and eat his lunch in peace. Perfectly content. His mind didn't wander to Belinda Kittridge and what she might be doing at that moment. Not even for a second. He held his plastic fork straight into the air, his lunch poised on top of his other palm. Not. For. A. Second. Bennett growled, cursing Jonas under his breath, and marched back into his office. It would be a lunch while working kind of day.

By the time the last piece of fish met its destiny, Bennett had spent an absurd amount of time reading the press Belinda and her family got for their benefits and other community work. Though they were mentioned in conjunction with other Portside families, it did seem to be as Bennett thought. They moved in their own circle, getting along but separate from the other families to a certain extent.

Belinda volunteered for various activities when she was in town, and she and her family contributed to an assortment of places and events in Portside and beyond, especially when it came to the arts and boating. In fact, Belinda and her grandmother had recently led an exclusive art-related fundraiser.

Where could he "naturally" run into her though? Bennett ran his fingers through his dark hair, contemplating the common denominators. There wasn't much of a way around it, he would have to watch her and create his own natural meeting place.

Chapter 5

True to his word, Kyle had bought no food of interest to her, but he had developed a sudden craving for all things homemade now that he had her captive. Belinda smiled to herself while strolling through the small downtown market. Kyle had started a list of things he wanted her to make while she was in town. Incredible. The man who couldn't keep track of his keys had made her a list—a legible one, mind you, with stars for bullet points, stuck on the fridge front and center. Oh well. He certainly appreciated her cooking by letting none of it go to waste, and her nana had advised her to use her skills for all they were worth. So she would. Besides, she'd learned that Jeff had been murdered, which she'd as much as told that detective, and it would help her de-stress to bake.

Rounding out the vegetables for the evening, Belinda headed for the baking aisle. Checking her list to make sure she didn't muse her way out of the store without something important, she glanced up to see the storm cloud eyes of That Guy from the party staring straight at her over the boxes of organic granola. Startled and embarrassed for no good reason, Belinda quickly averted her eyes and booked it to another aisle.

Just when she thought she was safe with the flour and semi-sweet chocolate chips, Jarrett materialized next to her, pouty faced and huffy. The band gig. She'd forgotten all about it in the craziness. And, honestly, she'd never intended to go and he as much as knew that. But, nevertheless, he was going to give her the Greenhouse Treatment, as Kyle called it. Jarrett would blast her with guilt to see if she'd grow useful to him.

Jarrett deigned to say hello to her and then stood there holding his bottle of soda, his cheeks suctioned in from repressing his loathing of her.

Belinda took a deep breath. Time to be the adult. "How was your gig yesterday?"

"You mean practice?"

Oops. Of course she meant practice. "Yes, practice. How did it go?"

"Awful."

"Oh. I'm sorry to hear that."

Jarrett shrugged.

So far, not so good, but he wasn't making any move to leave and Belinda was out of conversation starters. Just when she was about to come up with some clever out like, "Well, look at the time," That Guy rounded the corner behind Jarrett, walking straight toward her.

That was the good and bad news.

His expression was flat, but not blank. No, not blank at all when Belinda looked closely.

"I found them," That Guy said, shaking a box of—granola bars?—over his head.

Belinda glanced behind her to look for the receiving end of That Guy's dialogue, and stood in complete shock when he took her basket and positioned himself next to her like they were...together. Had she actually known this poor guy and totally forgotten he existed? Belinda took another look at him. No, she felt confident she wouldn't forget a guy that good-looking.

Jarrett got over his surprise and focused his sulking blue eyes on the man next to her.

"Ready?" That Guy said to Belinda. "We're running late." He slipped his hand through hers, gripping her fingertips. A bolt went through her and she nearly yanked away, but he kept too tight a grip.

Still unsure if it was a rescue or a trap leading to bigger problems, Belinda said a quick good-bye to Jarrett, who glared with all his might at That Guy, and followed her new companion across the store. He strode next to her like they walked through the grocery store together everyday, which she quickly decided had pros and cons.

Pro: he held her basket, which she realized too late would be way heavier by the end of her trip than she wanted.

Con: she had no idea how to get rid of him and he was walking super fast. What if he just got in the car with her and drove off?

She started to ask him who he was when he cut her off. "What else do we need?"

Still stunned, she glanced at her list and detoured to the refrigerated section, That Guy not missing a beat behind her. She filled up her basket, now really grateful she wasn't carrying it, and hustled to the checkout lines. Making it to her car and the finish line, so she hoped, her Worst Case Scenario actually happened.

That Guy snipped her keys from her fingertips and started the car. Belinda ran around to the other side to ensure he didn't leave without her. As she did so, Second Worst Case Scenario happened. Only this one never occurred to her before.

Lily Devore crawled up out of her silver convertible and looked directly at her, clearly taking note of the strange man in the driver's side of Belinda's car. Acting like they hadn't just made eye contact, Lily marched past her and into the store. Flustered, but with no time to think as her car revved, Belinda buckled in.

As soon as they started moving, he spoke. Finally. "We'll drive around the block and come back."

"Why?"

He glanced at her like the answer was obvious. "Because of the kid. It would look weird if we left separately."

We wouldn't want that, Belinda thought. "Personally, it looks weird that we left together. It's quite possible that Lily Devore will know your name before I do."

That Guy's lip twitched, a glint lighting up the back of his eyes. "Bennett Tate."

Repeating his name silently, Belinda realized that Bennett Tate already knew her. That thought unsettled her, especially considering she was now at his mercy in her car. He went straight through the next intersection, hung a right, then another right, and zipped back towards the market, coming to a stop under the shade of a tree near the road in the parking lot.

Before she could begin to ask all the questions flooding her mind, Bennett got out. "Enjoy your dinner," he said and started walking away.

"Pleasure meeting you!" Belinda called to him, but he didn't acknowledge her.

She watched him walk, hoping to get some clue about him other than that she'd seen him two mysterious times now. But Bennett Tate was not so easily decoded and he walked across the street and kept going.

Belinda took a deep breath to steady her nerves before she attempted to drive home. As she sat there wondering about her pretend friend, she couldn't decide if she was more disturbed by his hand holding or the fact that he left without so much as a glance back at her.

As with most things in Belinda's life, there was an upshot to the whole weird market experience: it gave Belinda a story for Victoria the next day and took her mind off her more immediate troubles.

"He sounds hot," Victoria said. "I'd go for a third encounter if I were you."

Belinda laughed. The two of them drove around town, scouting for a possible venue for Belinda's future cupcake boutique. The town of Portside had almost everything you needed—except fancy and scrumptious cupcakes. With encouragement and advice from her nana, Belinda had decided over the winter to use some of her money to fix that. "You don't think it's creepy?"

"Yeah, but it's also hot. Creepy hot."

Belinda kept a lookout for empty commercial space, afraid she'd miss something while yapping. "I'm scared that I'm going senile and I actually do know him."

Victoria shook her head. "You wouldn't forget a guy that attractive."

"You haven't even seen him!"

"I have a good imagination, and you would not forget a man that attractive." Victoria stopped to let a family cross the street. "You know, you keep acting like you have no recourse to find out who he is. You're a Kittridge. You know everybody in Portside and everybody knows you."

Portside was not a very big town, though it liked to fan out its feathers. It was tough to hide there.

"I hadn't thought of that." Belinda watched the woman push a baby carriage back onto the sidewalk. That would be Victoria soon enough.

Victoria grinned. "That's why I love you."

Belinda watched store after store go by, chewing on that.

"You should be near the Rusty Pirate," Victoria said, pointing. "People can go there for dinner and lunch and then cross into your boutique for dessert."

"There's also that sandwich place at the end of the shops. Best grilled cheese ever."

"But no trip to Portside is complete without—"

"Gelato!"

"I was going to say billiards in downtown, but sure, gelato."

Belinda's mouth turned down. "I stink at pool."

"You're not picking a location based on your skill levels. You're just trying to attract people who will want your cupcakes." Victoria winked and swung into an open spot on the street right across from the Rusty Pirate. "Time to taste test the recommendations."

They waited for the hostess to seat them and between the leaves of a palm tree, Belinda saw the glistening black hair of Lily Devore and across from her, Jarrett.

Belinda elbowed Victoria, moving out of the line of sight so Jarrett couldn't see her, yanking Victoria along with her. "Please, please tell me," Belinda whispered as they followed the hostess to their seat, "that he did not ask her out and she accepted."

Victoria climbed up onto the stool using the bar on the bottom as leverage. "I can't see that, can you?"

"Only if she's using him."

"What would Lily need him for? And don't say what you're really thinking because I am pregnant and might throw up on you."

Belinda scrunched her nose in disgust. "I'm not thinking that anyway. It wouldn't be like her. I actually don't know what to think."

They both tried to shrink into the shadows as much as possible as Lily left. She didn't even glance around, putting on her sunglasses and strutting off down the street, looking pleased about something. Jarrett left a minute later, walking in the opposite direction of Lily. Belinda glanced at Victoria. Odd. But first things first. Belinda had to unravel the mystery that was Bennett Tate. And she was formulating a plan.

Chapter 6

After contemplating how her family name might help her in her quest for the real Bennett Tate, Belinda just took the boring route and searched for him online. The only real glimmer of hope was in Tate Security, but with no photos of the owner, she couldn't be sure it was him. So Belinda had Victoria make an appointment under a false name. It might have been more of a ruse than necessary, but it was much more exciting than just calling Stellan.

Belinda turned in slow circles around the blank canvas of a bedroom in the upstairs of Victoria's house. Or, rather, the future nursery of Baby Hart. Victoria and Belinda had painted several strips of different colors side by side on the wall. With no shades on the windows, the sun hit the room at full force, practically blinding her.

"I know the color swatches are a little early." Victoria patted her still-flat tummy. "But I just couldn't wait."

She handed Belinda a glass of water and examined the rainbow of selections. On her bare feet, Victoria barely came up to Belinda's shoulders. Would their child be short and petite like her mother? Or tall and wiry like his dad?

"Does Dan have a color preference? I mean, despite the gender."

"He hates green, but that's all he's saying for the moment." Victoria leaned against the wall. "Just wait, though. As soon as it's time to buy the paint, he'll suddenly hate the color I've chosen. It never fails."

"I thought he had no opinions on these matters?"

Victoria laughed. "It's a myth, my dear. A total myth."

After doing all the damage they could in the nursery, they switched headquarters to the office on the first floor. Victoria scrolled through the items on Belinda's cousin's wedding registry online, zooming in on pieces here and there as she or Belinda pointed to things. As they got towards the end, both of them developed lemon faces.

"This is the saddest wedding registry I've ever laid eyes on," Victoria said. "Candle holders? Really?"

"I procrastinated and now all the good gifts are taken."

"Do they actually want a bread maker? I mean, does anyone actually use those things?"

Belinda slanted her eyes. "Don't you have a bread maker?"

"Yes, one of our wedding presents, and guess where it is?"

"The attic?"

"The attic. We used it once—maybe twice—right after we got married when we were excited to cook and clean and make fresh bread. But we would always remember that we could make bread when it was time to eat and then it was too late, so we finally gave up and heaved it into storage with the other rejected wedding gifts."

"The cappuccino maker would be fun."

"Belinda, I am not spending two-hundred dollars so the princess can have café-style cappuccino without changing out of her PJs."

Belinda sighed. "So what then? The forty-dollar iced tea pitcher?"

"We could buy them an ice pick."

"And you're complaining that nobody uses a bread maker?"

"Hey, there is more than one use for an ice pick." Victoria grinned. "Could come in handy past the honeymoon period."

"Yes, let's buy the happy couple their future murder weapon."

The doorbell rang, making them both jump. Victoria snickered and skipped out of the room, winking as she partially closed the office door. Showtime. Belinda could hear talking from the front room and tiptoed to peek through the crack in the door.

Victoria shook hands with a tall guy with dark brown hair in a sweater over a collared shirt and jeans. Well, that proved it. Bennett Tate owned Tate Security. Now what? Belinda frowned. She hadn't thought this all the way through. The phone rang and Victoria excused herself, floating off to the kitchen.

Belinda stepped away from the door, her sneaker squeaking on the wood floor. She winced, keeping perfectly still. After a few seconds, she relaxed. Then the door swung open and Bennett stood on the threshold. Belinda's face turned the color of pink tulips as his mouth turned up and gray eyes glistened.

Busted.

When the head spinning passed and Bennett's face came into focus, his gray eyes the color of those funny dogs with a weird name that are famous because of a photographer, he expected her to do something. Then she realized he had stretched out his hand. *My he has hairy arms,* she thought, but he actually gave her hand a firm shake instead of the half-hearted business most people offered.

"Tell me about Victoria's party plans," Bennett said, his eyes glinting.

"Oh...well, there isn't much to say really. I imagine there will be a few people here. Or, a lot since she's hiring you. Your company that is. To do security." Belinda glanced at the kitchen. What was Victoria doing?

"So this isn't a joint affair?" he said sarcastically.

So that's how it was going to be. Belinda slanted her eyes. "Do you work parties a lot?"

Bennett shrugged. "A few here and there. It's mostly more official events." He crooked one bushy eyebrow. "Are you planning something too?"

"You'd be the first to know." Belinda flushed. "I mean...you come well recommended."

Bennett's eyes glinted all the more. *Well, enjoy it, gray-eyed eagle,* Belinda thought. Eventually, when she regained her wits, he'd have a hard time keeping up.

Cliffhanger

"The murder hasn't put you off?" he said. At first, Belinda thought he was attempting to make light of things, but between his tone and expression, especially the lack of luster in his eyes, he was obviously concerned that it would.

She swallowed, feeling her pants for non-existent pockets. "You did your job and that may not have even happened when you were there." Belinda's stomach churned thinking how close she had been to an actual murder. "Plus, you weren't the only person in the house."

"True. But most of the people were in the living room, and with the music so loud and the waves crashing, I doubt anyone would have heard if he—" Bennett stopped in his tracks, aware that Belinda's eyes had about doubled in size. He shook his head. "It doesn't matter."

Belinda smiled, fascinated and disturbed simultaneously. "You sound like a police detective. In fact, you were once, weren't you? I read it on your site."

The light returned to his eyes. "You looked at my website?"

"Mostly your bio." Belinda felt her face grow hot again. Why couldn't she censor better? And, furthermore, why did he have to enjoy it so much? "Why did you leave? You seem like you're made for the job."

Bennett shifted his gaze to the side. "I like the puzzles. I don't like the politics. Let's leave it at that."

"So how did you get into security?" In the back of her mind, Belinda knew that Victoria had disappeared for quite a long time.

"Primarily because of happenstance. I did some private investigating work with Parker—"

"The detective who interviewed me?"

Bennett half-smiled. "That's him. A client asked if we did security. Jonas wasn't interested, but I liked the sounds of it, and one thing led to another and eventually I retired from the force and started Tate Security full-time."

"Do you ever miss it? The police work?"

"I never made it to Jonas' position so I'd have to say no. Most of what we did was tedious and boring. The private investigating was a smidge better, but—" He cut himself off. "It was still dull."

Belinda doubted the "but" in that sentence was supposed to lead to a repeat of the previous one. "So security isn't boring?"

The little flicker came back into his eyes. "Not right now."

Belinda's heart rate picked up. "Well, I'm glad. That you're not bored. Right now." She clasped her hands, pressing them together to try and stop the rambling.

Victoria materialized, looking pleased as punch, a twinkle in her hazel eyes.

Bennett crossed his arms and looked down at both of them like two naughty students in his class. "Am I hired, or should I assume the party's a charade, Mrs. Victoria Hart?"

Victoria looked surprised. "How did you—?"

"Your names are out front on one of the garden gnomes."

"I forgot about that," she whispered guiltily to Belinda.

Bennett half-smiled.

"You wouldn't tell me anything," Belinda said in a huff. "You're at Stellan's party, but clearly not for that reason. You act like I should know you at the market. I thought I was going nuts. How else was I supposed to find out who you are?"

"You could ask."

Belinda's eyes flashed, gold flecks shining like the lights on the bridge at night. "You should have your photo on the website!"

"Why? This is much more interesting. Maybe a waste of time, but still."

"I am not a waste of time, sir." Belinda stood with her hands on her hips, stretching to her full height. "I'm a Kittridge."

Victoria glanced from Belinda to Bennett.

"You have a paint smudge on your nose," he said matter-of-factly. "And I never said you were a waste of my time."

Belinda's eyes widened and he excused himself with a smile on his lips and left while Belinda ran to the bathroom. "Why didn't you tell me I had a pink paint smudge on my nose?"

"Calm down, Kittridge. It's not that bad."

"Not that bad!" Belinda pointed at the tip of her nose. Right on top of her ski jump was a strawberry pink smear. "Honestly! Every moment of my life since I got back has been a scene from a sitcom."

"It's not just since you got back, hon."

Belinda glared.

"So I was totally right about him." Victoria leaned against the door frame. "I don't think you need to worry about seeing him again. He's going to work it out one way or another."

Belinda shrugged. "So what if he does? It doesn't mean I want to see him." She scrubbed her nose, but it only grew red with pink icing.

"Don't even bother playing that card with me. I know you're anything but indifferent."

"If I didn't have to think about Baby Hart, I would whack you in the face with a throw pillow. You're a terrible best friend."

"What are you talking about? I'm an awesome best friend. I just got you your third encounter with Hot Security Guy."

"You can tell yourself that as the evening news cuts to an unflattering candid of me reporting that I'm missing."

"Would you feel better if I choose a flattering candid of you?"

Belinda rolled her eyes up to the ceiling. "Maybe."

Victoria smiled. "So that was exciting. What do we do next?"

Belinda gave up and dried her face off. "I think I should talk with Stellan. He's always in the know."

"You want to see if he knows anything about Jarrett?"

Belinda dabbed her nose with the towel. "I'm worried about him. He's been really upset since I got back."

"He's a kid. He doesn't get it—yet."

"As true as that may be, it doesn't mean he won't do something completely stupid. Besides, Lily's acting all kinds of suspicious."

"I think that may just be her nature."

"Well, nature or not, I want to know what she's up to."

Chapter 7

That's not the way Bennett planned on going, but the one-way lane he'd wanted to take while trailing Belinda was blocked off because of a house demolition, so he took a longer route along the cobblestones and onto the main loop through town. Bearing right into the nucleus of shops and places to eat, Bennett took a sharp left up a different one-way street to turn back the direction he actually wanted to go.

Squeezing past the parked cars on a road that was barely larger than an alley, he rose to the peak where it curved left and dipped back down. In the cemetery nestled amid the townhouses, he made out two people talking in the shade. One of those people was Belinda Kittridge. Bennett pulled up the next street and parked cockeyed, jogging back to the cemetery. He hung around just before the wrought-iron fence protecting the graveyard, straining to hear. He hadn't been able to get a good look at her companion, but Belinda was still talking rapidly. She sounded frantic.

"This is going to open up everything," she whispered harshly. "It's probably connected, and that means we...all of us will be suspects."

"I still don't know what you want me to do about it."

Bennett listened closely while pretending to check something on his phone, but his head shot up instantly when he heard his client talking—Stellan Mayhew. Bennett's brow furrowed trying to put that together.

"I just want to know what actually happened that day," Belinda said. "You two haven't told us the whole truth."

"Why do you think we've been lying? You and Kyle constantly seem to forget that Mark was our friend too. And we were just as upset and just as frustrated as you."

Belinda was quiet. Bennett's mind had been racing to figure out the topic of their conversation, but now he knew. They were talking about the sailing accident.

"You could just as easily know something I don't," Stellan said.

Bennett could hear the surprise, or even alarm, in Belinda's silence, but she recovered quickly.

"I wasn't there."

"But you saw him before, didn't you? Or am I not supposed to know that?"

Bennett strained to hear as a car passed.

"...not meant to be a secret."

"But it was," Stellan said, "even after. You never came out with it."

"What was the point?" Now she sounded angry. "It was just as well that no one knew."

"So you wouldn't have to go head-to-head with Lily?" Stellan snorted. "You're afraid of her, just like Mark."

"I am not afraid of her, and neither was he."

"Prove it."

There was a pause as if Belinda was deciding how to respond. "Mark broke up with her."

Bennett worked to keep pace, but it was tough not knowing the point of their debate.

"Did Lily know that?"

Bennett was pretty sure Belinda scowled. "I think you're confusing Mark with yourself."

Bennett raised his eyebrows. She had an acidic undercurrent to her, didn't she?

Cliffhanger

"And I think you're confusing Mark with the hero he's been played up to be since he died." Stellan's tone turned venomous. "Turns out he was just as imperfect as the rest of us when he slipped and cracked his skull open on the deck of his own boat."

Bennett heard a thwack, and realized Belinda slapped Stellan.

"If you hadn't been smashed," Belinda choked out, "you would have been able to save him!"

Stellan was quiet long enough for Bennett to wonder if he'd left. But then he spoke, and he sounded weary. "No one could have saved him, Belinda. Not even you."

Bennett heard crunching and when no more conversation was forthcoming, he figured they'd split. He walked over to the fence, taking a cautious peek. Belinda was huddled under a tree, her face hidden but body convulsing from sobs. Bennett turned to leave, but couldn't just walk away with her like that.

"Hey!" he said through the fence. It seemed rude, but it was easy to fake just walking by that way. "Are you all right?"

Belinda stood up with a jerk, hastily wiping her face with her sleeves. "I'm fine." She stayed under the tree, looking ready to bolt the other direction.

Bennett wrapped his fingers through the fence posts, the metal sending a shock of cold up his arms. "Can I help?"

Belinda took a hesitant step forward, coming out of the shadow of the tree. She looked like a scared rabbit. "I doubt it."

"Try me." Bennett forced one corner of his mouth up. Smiling put people at ease, right?

"I'm...I'm just scared by everything that's happened."

"Do you want to talk about it?"

Belinda's eyes went to the ground, processing his question. "Maybe later."

Well, it was worth a try. Bennett shrugged casually.

Belinda took another step toward the fence. "You always seem to be here for the catastrophes."

"Well, you know, you're like a type of car."

Belinda's eyes narrowed.

"I—I mean, I'm like a type of car." He struggled to remember the metaphor Jonas had used. "You've never seen me before and now...now you see me...all the time." Bennett felt his neck grow hot under his collar. This is why he preferred to keep quiet.

Belinda approached the fence, placing her hands above his on the posts. Her brown eyes started to regain some of their golden sparkle. "I have no idea what you're talking about, but thank you for wanting to help."

Bennett swallowed. "Would you like me to walk you back to your car or something?"

"What kind of 'or something' do you have in mind?"

Bennett just threw that in there without thinking about it. He didn't have a response planned. "The kind that includes pastries?"

Belinda laughed. "Thank you. I'd like it if you walked me back to my car."

Bennett nodded and waited patiently for her to walk back around. They strolled along, Belinda gazing off thoughtfully. "Mark is buried at that cemetery," she said after several minutes. "It's Jeff's murder, you know? It's taking us all back there."

Bennett fought to think of something to say that wasn't what he wanted to say. He couldn't let her know he'd heard her conversation with Stellan, but his curiosity wanted to get the better of him.

"Do you have any moment in your life that you just wish you could do over with what you know now?" she said.

Bennett got the feeling she was talking about Mark again. But which moment in particular? He hated to acknowledge the one thing that immediately came to his own mind. "Honestly, more than one. But, yeah."

Belinda stopped and turned to face him, her arms wrapped around her body and eyes red from crying. A breeze rolled up the street and Bennett inhaled the fresh smell of spring. Even the red and blue and yellow houses flanking them, hundreds of years old, looked like they stood a little taller next to a tree in bud. Belinda dug her toe between bricks on the sidewalk.

"I have something I wish I could do over," Belinda said softly. Bennett tuned out the spring air and general good feeling of the world around him, positive she was about to reveal something important. "I went to get something I'd left on Mark's boat the night before he died, and—"

A car broke into her speech, but instead of passing, it careened to a stop right next to them. Jarrett's head popped out of the driver's side. Bennett steamed, his face blackening as Jarrett's teeth flashed in a smile. He wanted to bulldoze the kid's car with his SUV.

Unlike at the market, Jarrett pretended like Bennett wasn't even remotely an obstacle to his romancing Belinda and ignored Bennett's glacier stare. Either the kid was running on hormones or he was really happy about something. Belinda tensed, rubbing the back of her neck, as Jarrett chatted, perfectly oblivious to her discomfort.

As soon as the kid paused to take a breath, blabbing on about the new song his band was trying to learn, Bennett jumped in. "I think we better move on." Belinda's eyes betrayed relief when she met his, and a joy Bennett couldn't quite understand swelled inside of him.

"Are you late again?" Jarrett spat. Apparently, he'd met his happiness quotient for the day.

Bennett wrapped his arm around Belinda, slipping his fingers around her hip, and shot a smile Jarrett's way. Belinda seemed to regain some of her usual verve and stood up a little straighter. "I'm sorry,

Jarrett. I need to get back to packing. With everything that's happened, I'm dragging my heels on it."

Jarrett's eyes softened and he nodded. "Yeah, I get that. You've got to get ready for the demo and all." He paused, probably hoping to draw out the conversation more, but Belinda wasn't biting. "I'll catch you later then." With one more cold look at Bennett, Jarrett sped off.

Bennett could feel Belinda relax next to him. "You've been polishing your armor, haven't you?" she said.

"You shouldn't apologize."

"To who?"

"To Jarrett. He's being a pest and ignoring the fact that you're uncomfortable with his attention."

Belinda looked surprised. "He's only—"

"He's old enough to stalk you."

"He hasn't been stalking me." Belinda glanced at him reprovingly.

"He seems to show up everywhere you are."

"He lives next door."

Bennett shrugged. "It's still odd."

"About as odd as, let's say, you showing up at every turn? And I can't say you live anywhere near me." Belinda folded her arms, her eyes back to normal.

She was smart, and catching on. Bennett liked that.

He decided to take the conversation down a different street. "Do I make you uncomfortable?"

Surprise lit up her eyes. "I haven't decided yet."

"Then maybe I should give you more time."

Belinda's arms dropped and she rubbed the tip of her finger. "Just as long as you don't kidnap me again."

Bennett smirked, falling into pace with her down the sidewalk. "Where were we? Before Jarrett interrupted us?" Bennett knew exactly where they were, but he wanted to give her a chance to volunteer.

Belinda's face look troubled. "I...I can't recall."

So much for that. Bennett guessed that he and Jarrett were now even after the market incident. It made no difference. She'd now given away that she welcomed his presence, so he wasn't about to disappoint her.

~ * ~

Victoria took several turns down side streets the next afternoon, heading towards Lily's house. They went uphill, Belinda putting down her window to inhale the salt air. In an enclave beyond where most people traveled, Lily's family's house was nestled behind a gate. Belinda wanted to check it out to learn why she was back in Portside—and what she might want with a kid like Jarrett.

"So we just watch to see what happens?" Victoria said, biting into a candy bar. "What if she doesn't leave?"

Belinda shrugged.

"What if you can't get inside if she does leave? Unlike your house, this woman appears to be serious about her security. And they have a much bigger gate and wall than you guys do."

Belinda sighed. "This might be a complete waste of time."

"Nonsense. You're a Kittridge, remember?"

Belinda cringed. "I actually said that, didn't I?"

"Yep." Victoria licked chocolate from her fingers. "But he enjoyed it immensely."

"Do you really think that?"

"Absolutely. He basically said so himself. After all, you, Belinda Kittridge," Victoria dropped her voice an octave, "are never a waste of time." She pondered that. "You know, I bet he knew it was us all along."

"And he still came?"

"Why not? He'd get to see you."

Belinda didn't want to admit it right then, but she kind of liked that idea.

After close to an hour of twirling her hair, discussing possible names for Belinda's shop, and eating one of Victoria's candy bars, the gate finally slid open and Lily zipped out of her driveway in her silver convertible. Belinda and Victoria hunched over as she passed, just hoping Lily didn't see them. As soon as she'd disappeared around the bend, Belinda jumped out of the car.

"Keep watch!" she said before slamming the door.

Victoria watched as Belinda squeaked through the gate before it trapped her inside. Belinda caught her breath and marched around to the back entrance, peering inside where it was dark and empty. She found a side window open and with a little pressure, popped the screen out and climbed through. Belinda dashed up the stairs to find Lily's bedroom. Not that she knew what she was looking for. Just any clues to what Lily's ulterior motive could be for coming back to Portside. Notes, tickets, receipts. Anything.

Belinda found the room she suspected belonged to Lily. She glanced out the window and all she could see was sky—and the occasional head bobbing along the Ocean Walk beyond the backyard. The house was insanely quiet except for the chatter of walkers blown up by the wind.

After peeking into a few dresser drawers, Belinda found an envelope buried under some clothes. Money? She pulled it out out of curiosity. Inside was a thick stack of photographs. Belinda flipped through them, the first few just of Mark.

Belinda sighed. He had been a handsome guy. Bronze year-round like Kyle with milk chocolate brown hair that had the slightest bit of curl at the ends. And blue eyes. But not light blue like most people. They were dark like indigo. She wondered what he would look like now. Where he would be. Who he would be with...

The stack slipped from her grasp, all one-hundred photos splaying out onto the wood floor. Belinda panicked, trying to corral them with her palms when she caught glimpses of herself in a couple of the photos. Then she noticed she was in several of them. Looking closer, she realized she was in almost every single photograph, except the first few.

Her heart raced. There were photos at different times of the day in different locations on different days with one common denominator: Mark. Mark was with her in every photo.

Then Victoria whistled.

It was the signal they'd used years ago when doing things they shouldn't have been doing. Belinda frantically gathered the photos, sticking two down her waistband. She stuffed the envelope back where she found it and slammed the dresser shut, flying out of the room and down the stairs and back out the side window, hastily setting the screen back in place.

Belinda ran straight for the edge of the property toward the Ocean Walk. She turned sideways to sidle between two tall bushes that acted as a fence, getting entangled in the branches and finally pushing and pulling herself free on the other side and hopped down. Belinda spun around, not sure which way to go and headed to her left. She could walk to the next street entrance and circle back around.

She speed-walked in that direction, hoping Victoria had not driven home since Belinda didn't even have a cell phone with her. She almost tripped going down some stone steps and at the end, standing under one of the low-lying arches, was Bennett Tate.

"You!" she blurted out. "What are you doing here?" She had hoped to sound casual, but failed from the startled look in his eyes.

Bennett surveyed her, either confused or annoyed by her appearance. He got up close, his lips pulled tight and eyes hard, and reached his hand toward her. Belinda held her breath and tilted back. He plucked a leaf from her hair and brought it up near his eyes, twirling it. Belinda's eyes went wide, envisioning what she must look like after fighting with the bush. Her hands automatically went to her head, feeling for the damage. Of course, what could be worse than the paint smudge on her nose?

"Been in the woods?" he said.

Belinda laughed rather unintentionally, stopped herself, and tried to answer rationally. "My hair must have gotten caught in one of the overhanging bushes. You know, along some of the walls that kind of stick out." Bennett's expression didn't let on whether he believed her. "Are you out for a walk?"

Bennett tucked the leaf into his palm but stayed a mere breath away. He looked pretty much the way he had the day before, except he'd skipped shaving, which, naturally, only made him hotter. Meantime, she looked like Bush Woman. "I'm thinking," he said. "But I like to walk when I do that."

"Thinking about what?"

Bennett's gray eyes held that little spark in the back. She might have missed it, but he was standing so close. "I was thinking about your unfortunate friend." He aimed the leaf in the direction of the cliffs jutting out beyond the ones they stood on.

"He was unfortunate," Belinda said, regaining some calmness. She licked her lips, rough on her tongue, and dropped her eyes. "I...I have to go. My friend is waiting for me." She tucked hair behind her ears that blocked her vision and stepped to the side to walk around Bennett who blocked her path. She squeezed her back to the stone to pass him. "It was nice meeting you again!" She jogged toward the street entrance, praying he didn't follow her.

Thankfully, Victoria was on her wavelength and waited for her in the turnaround by one of the Walk's entrances. Victoria looked horrified as Belinda crashed in the passenger's seat. "What happened to you?"

Belinda flipped open the visor mirror and shrieked. "I just stood there talking to a man looking like this!"

"What kind of man?"

Belinda pursed her lips.

"Well, your level of panic should coincide with the person who saw you. Now, if it was someone who's friends with your father, do you really care that much how you looked? No, of course not. So what kind of man are we talking about?"

Belinda wanted to cry. "The kind that we trick into coming to your house."

It took Victoria a second, but then she lit up. "I'm sure he didn't notice your appearance." She did a three-point turn and pulled out to the main road.

Belinda grimaced. "I'm positive it was the total opposite. He pulled a leaf from my hair and then asked if I'd been in the woods."

"What did you do anyway?"

Belinda explained her foray through the perimeter bushes and then how Bennett was walking toward her. For the moment, she decided to keep the photos to herself.

"So what did you tell him you were doing?"

"I'm not sure I ever got around to it. I sort of unintentionally turned the conversation on him." Belinda tossed leaves out the window as they drove.

"I guess you remembered the whistle?"

"Summer before senior year. Saved by the whistle as my father showed up while Matt Reardon mouth attacked me on our non-date though I was supposed to be at the movies with you."

"Saved you on two accounts."

"Matt Reardon. Can you believe I spent an entire school year daydreaming about him? Then I finally get close to all my dreams coming true, and all I wanted to do the entire night was kill him. Came this close to pushing him overboard when he tried to kiss me."

"Hormones, darling. We all had them."

"At least your infatuations made sense. Every boy I liked in high school turned out to be a plague upon mankind."

"It's a good thing you left them all behind. Now you're free for Hot Security Man."

Belinda shifted her eyes sideways.

"Just sayin', I don't think he's a plague upon mankind."

"Not yet."

"You're older now. You can spot the plagues before you get emotionally invested." Victoria winked, detouring downhill toward downtown on the divided four lane road.

As she pushed down on the brakes nearing a red light, Victoria glanced in her rearview mirror to see a car barreling toward them.

Chapter 8

Bennett watched in horror as the car that had just cut in front of him bashed into the black Fiat, sending it careening through the intersection and straight for the corner of a shop. Fear and panic replaced his idle wondering what Belinda had done inside that house and why. He ran toward the smashed Fiat, grateful he'd followed them from the Ocean Walk.

He yelled at the dazed shop owner to call for help, swinging Belinda's door open. "Can either of you hear me?" he said. He thought Belinda moaned and her friend didn't make a peep. He couldn't help them and just stood there in frustration, waiting for the paramedics.

Belinda's eyes flickered as Bennett finally heard sirens. Fortunately, one of the police stations was not far away. Belinda and Victoria started to come to as the help arrived and Bennett was forced out of the picture as the police moved in and the paramedics braced up the two women and helped them into the ambulances. Belinda was in good hands and he made sure that they knew where to get in touch with Kyle before they whisked them away to the hospital.

Bennett glanced around as they drove off, catching sight of a camera under the overhang of the shop's roof. His eyes widened and he scrambled to get to the owner, whom he knew. The poor guy just stood in disbelief where the nose of the Fiat stabbed through the side of his shop.

"Is that camera working?" Bennett said, his arm stretched up at the device.

"Y–yes." The gray-haired man blinked like he answered before he truly understood the question. "Oh...oh!" He did a three-sixty in place and waved Bennett into the flower shop and toward the back where the camera connected to a computer. "I see what you want." He scuttled out of the way so Bennett could take a seat. "This thing might have seen the accident."

Bennett nodded while he clicked on the mouse, rewinding the footage to just minutes earlier. His heart raced waiting for them to come into view. The shop owner gripped the back of the seat, bending over, watching with the same fixated horror as he got to see how the car landed in his front window. Bennett rewound.

"That truck hit those two girls on purpose!" Mr. Trebor said in shock.

Bennett zoomed and froze on the truck that hit them. The camera caught it sideways, but other shop cameras on the strip may have gotten clearer footage.

Bennett watched it again with Jonas minutes later, knowing he would regret telling Jonas about trailing Belinda. But he might as well get it over with. Jonas would be all over that sooner or later.

"I don't know what Belinda found," Bennett said. "But I'm positive it freaked her out."

"How did you come across this anyway?"

Bennett hesitated. If he told the truth, he'd never hear the end of it. "I...I've been following her."

Jonas' grin transitioned into a bittersweet smile. "I'll find out how they're doing after this."

Bennett wanted to sigh in relief. Well, he could do that when he got home. "Thank you."

"You're welcome. We're checking around the intersection to see if there's any hope of other cameras filming the accident."

Bennett nodded vigorously. "I think there's an excellent chance of that. I've consulted with some of the businesses here and recommended outdoor cameras."

"If any of them listened to you, I'd be tempted to marry you."

"It's not mutual."

Jonas chuckled. "Fine. What if I said that Belinda would be tempted to marry you?" All Jonas could hear was some sort of grunt or growl. "We've got this. So," Jonas said, leaving his people to collect the video footage from Mr. Trebor, "you did your own little surveillance on Fawn Eyes, eh?"

Bennett wanted to groan.

Jonas smiled. "Why not? You started stalking her at the party. May as well keep going."

"I did not stalk her."

"All right, all right. Stalking carries ugly connotations. Let's say...observing." Jonas and Bennett marched out of the back of the building by the dumpsters. "You know what's weird?"

"You?"

Jonas snorted. "As if I would take your word on that. But seriously. So far almost no one at that party saw Jeff. Unless they're all lying, he wasn't ever a part of the actual event. He was completely MIA."

Bennett scratched his chin. He needed to shave. "I get the feeling that Jeff didn't go there for the party itself. Something else was afoot."

"Well, we have Jeff who had been gone for years. And apparently Lily Devore is the same thing. Then there's the Kittridges. But they all manage to be around for this seemingly random party."

"And the first two are connected to Mark Nichols and the infamous sailing accident."

"So are Fawn Eyes and her brother."

Bennett's eyes shot open briefly.

"Her brother sailed with those guys and Belinda herself had an unpleasant history with Jeff." Jonas squinted into the horizon. "I think I need to dig deeper into this sailing accident. It's looking like a core ingredient."

"And Belinda?"

Jonas eyed his friend in amusement. "Calm down. Fawn Eyes is not on my hit list. I wouldn't sick her on you if I thought she was homicidal."

Bennett frowned.

"Oh, boy," Jonas said. "I've got you thinking with that remark, haven't I?" Jonas lingered by his car, jangling his keys. "Belinda doesn't remind me of...you know who...not even a little bit."

"We're not in high school," Bennett said. "You can say her name."

"Mmm...I'd call her something, but it wouldn't be her name."

Bennett peeked around, lowering his voice. "When I'm with Belinda, I don't hesitate at all. That's what scares me."

"Yeah, I know. You save the frowny face and freaking out for me."

Bennett furrowed his brows. "I do not freak out."

"Oh yes, you do. You may not say much, but I know your mind's whirring." Jonas nodded at a fellow officer passing by. "Nothing says you have to go all raging bull on this. Part of the reason you got into such hot water before was because you made a snap judgment, and it was wrong."

"Thanks."

"Hey, you know that better than I do. So don't make a snap decision this time. Get to know her...progressively. If Belinda's not the charming pixie we both think she is right now, time will show her up."

"I have trouble with...progressive."

"Yeah, I know that too."

Bennett pushed a pebble around with his foot, hoping the ambulances had arrived at the hospital already. "She's surprised me from the start, and it hasn't stopped. That's the only reason I'm even considering it."

"You can't write people off just because of their, you know, class or whatever. One bad apple, etcetera."

Bennett digested that. Jonas was usually right about these things. "So...progressively?"

"Progressively. You can do it; I have faith in you."

Bennett grunted.

"Back to the more official side of things, we found evidence on Jeff's body that he may have been in a fight recently."

"Really? Did you find bruising?"

"Better. Some blood under his fingernails."

"He grappled with his opponent then."

"What about her brother? Kyle?" Jonas said. "He was in with this whole group, and with Jeff Clark back in town, it seems likely he would have shown up at the party despite history."

"Kittridge is not on camera at any time, and I've spoken to Finn and Rachel and neither of them spotted Kyle."

Jonas sighed. "It's a real annoyance that you didn't have guys outside for this one."

"You can take that up with my client."

"I may have to. It's convenient that he didn't hire you for that on a night someone gets killed on his property." Jonas thought about that. "You could get more about Mayhew's history—all of them no doubt—from Belinda."

Bennett frowned.

"Don't look so irritated. Deep down, you know you're thrilled to have an excuse to talk to her again. And you should bring her something, flowers for example, because of the accident."

Bennett peeked up at Jonas. "Should I?"

"If you value her good opinion, then yes, you should." He clapped his hands together. "Divide and conquer. I handle the official interviews, and you keep chitchatting with the lovely insider. We're bound to figure out how this guy wound up on the bottom of a long drop."

Bennett arched an eyebrow. He wanted to argue Jonas' constant references to Belinda's physical appearance, but with images of her from his afternoon meeting on the Ocean Walk flashing into his mind, he found himself at a loss for words.

~ * ~

Kyle speed-walked down the corridor, his sneaker squeaking on the white linoleum. The smell hit him first. Rubbing alcohol and strong cleaners cutting into his sinuses. He zigzagged around nurses holding charts and pushing laptops, finally reaching the desk in the ER after sidestepping a boy on a stretcher guarded by two police officers. He glanced around to see if he could find Belinda, but fixed his eyes on the desk after glimpsing a woman behind a green and white curtain with tubes protruding from her nose.

He blinked sweat and grime from his eyes and tried to focus on the nurse in front of him. She pointed to the glass cubicle where he'd find his sister. It felt like the kind of place where you would most definitely try to escape from in a sci-fi movie.

"What happened?" Kyle flailed his arms out. For a second, he clearly resembled his twin sister. Belinda held her head, the throbbing that had just started to tone down returning. She put a finger to her lips to tell him to quiet down. "Sorry, but I've been panicking since they called me. Are you hurt?"

"Not seriously. I guess I blacked out briefly, but it must not be fatal because they're letting me go soon." Belinda paused. Talking only increased the headache. "I'm worried about Victoria."

Kyle sat down near the bed, calmer now. "I saw Dan on my way in and he said she's all right. So what happened?"

"I don't really know. One minute, we're laughing about something and then Vix screamed and we're flying into a store."

"You hit a store?"

"I think that's what it was but they tell me I have a mild concussion, so maybe it wasn't."

Kyle placed his wrist on her forehead.

"What are you doing?"

"I don't know. I just feel like I need to do something and that's all I can think of right now."

Belinda batted her brown eyes. "You could adjust my pillow. My head has hurt too much to bother, but it's hitting my neck funny." Belinda leaned forward so Kyle could move the pillow around.

"Better?"

"Much." Belinda managed a crooked smile.

"What do you feel like for dinner?"

"Pizza."

"Then pizza it is." Kyle paused. "You know, Mom and Dad are not going to believe all of this."

"Were we going to tell them?"

"I don't know. You're the responsible one."

"So that means I'm the one who gets to ruin their trip?"

"Of course not. We're in this together."

Belinda did not like that response. "Last time you said that, I wound up grounded. Alone."

Kyle grinned in his goofy way. "I remember that. That's when we snuck out to go to that concert during finals when we were on lockdown. Who did we go to see?"

"I don't even remember now, which proves just how so not worth it it was."

"And James Lavallee. Was he worth it?"

Belinda wanted to roll her eyes, but knew it would hurt too much. "That night was the first and last time I got grounded to be near James Lavallee."

Kyle snickered. "I gave you fair warning about that one, so you can't blame me." Kyle's cheekbones tightened and he reached out and gripped her forearm. "You deserve better, Bels. Much, much better."

Belinda assumed he meant James Lavallee and nodded her head weakly, feeling an urgent need to close her eyes again.

"I'm going to look after you, I promise." Belinda thought she heard him say something else about nothing bad happening to her, but it sounded far away as Belinda faded back into sleep.

Chapter 9

Belinda had no idea what it meant to find all those photographs of her with Mark in Lily's dresser, and she'd forgotten she even stuffed them in her pants until they fell out when she changed after returning from the hospital. Her body creaked and groaned when she woke up that morning and she felt like she'd been run over by a truck.

Ironically, it was almost true.

Kyle stayed home that morning to make sure she was all right to be alone, but had to go into work that afternoon, putting her on lockdown for the rest of the day. He wouldn't be back for hours and Belinda wasn't sure she should tell him about the photos just yet anyway. Nor did she have the physical or emotional strength to bother.

Physically, she and Victoria came out of the ordeal in okay shape. A little concussed with some scrapes and bruises, but that was all. Emotionally, Belinda felt rocked to her core. She always imagined her life flashing before her eyes in an event like that, but she didn't even have time. It was over before she saw the need for a flashback. When it came down to it, though, she only really cared about Victoria and her baby. She wanted to rip apart the person who hit them for Victoria's sake.

After staying curled up in bed for hours to watch a stream of cooking shows and taking mental notes of recipes to search online for later, Belinda finally showered. She'd expected the "wing" they lived in to be completely barren, but her mom had left a basket in her bathroom (she and Kyle had separates, thank goodness) of toiletries and brand spanking new towels made from Egyptian cotton. Wrapped in the pink terry-cloth bathrobe also left in her wardrobe, she twisted her hair up into a messy bun just as the doorbell rang.

Belinda padded downstairs, gripping the rail. They warned her that she'd experience dizziness for a while, but Belinda still wasn't quite prepared for it. Peering into the peephole, she hoped it wasn't the detective again. She took a step back. No, it was much worse than that. How did Bennett Tate find her? Belinda opened the door a crack, quickly running through any excuses that would work to keep from having to let him inside.

She smiled broadly, involuntarily checking her hair to make sure it was still in place. Thank goodness she'd showered...now she just needed to put on clothes.

One side of Bennett's mouth curled up and his eyes scanned her, finally settling on her eyes with a look Belinda thought was approval and maybe relief. They stared at each other for a minute, and he pushed a white pastry box into her hands. "I hope you like éclairs," he said.

Belinda nodded, all of the reasons to refuse to let him in flying from her head. After all, she didn't want to seem rude and he'd gone to the trouble to buy pastries. She wanted to fly upstairs to change, but she could only poke one step at a time and found it even difficult to pick out clothes, her mind wandering off of its task every few seconds. She finally managed to get dressed and make it safely down the stairs for the third time that day with Bennett waiting at the bottom poised to catch her if she fell.

"Are you all right?" he said, concern passing through his eyes as she recovered from her exertion.

"Oh, I'm all right." Belinda sat down on the bottom step. Just until Bennett became one whole person again instead of two or three hologram-looking beings.

He crouched down, scanning her face.

"It's just the—consequences—of the concussion. I'll be okay in a sec." Once she felt more focused, she stood slowly and Bennett trailed her to the back deck.

"How's your friend?"

"About the same as me." She involuntarily glanced at the water. "Nothing major." Belinda looked down at her hands, realizing they were starting to shake, and stuck them behind her back. "She's having a baby, you know."

Bennett nodded slowly.

"I was told you were there when the accident happened," Belinda said. "I wonder if it's your voice that I heard. It's all really fuzzy, but I remember someone asking me if I was okay."

"It could have been me. I was right behind you and got out to help."

"So you must have left the Ocean Walk right after I did."

Bennett replied with some vague answer and then shaded his eyes to get a good look at their view and nodded in approval. "Nice location. I like the gambrel roofs." He traced the shape in the air with his finger.

Belinda's eyes lit up. "You know roofs?"

Bennett's eyes glinted. "I know a little something about architecture."

That got Belinda's attention. Bennett Tate was unfolding like origami. Deceptively simple on the surface. "I'd say thank you, but I had nothing to do with it. Do you live on the water?" It was a stupid question, but Bennett didn't seem to care.

"Technically. But I have to drive or walk to see it."

"It's a good thing we're surrounded by water then. You don't have to go nearly so far. I've been farther inland for too long and I couldn't stand it any longer." Belinda wanted to sink into the turf as she rambled on about nonsense and hoped she didn't sound like the snob she felt like. "So I presume you came by for something more than chitchat. Can I help you somehow?"

Bennett pulled a leaf out of his pocket, twirling it the same way he had the day before. That dratted leaf. He knew. No wonder he was in security, nothing slipped his notice.

Bennett drew in close, the tip of his nose almost touching hers. Belinda's heart flip-flopped, and she was pretty certain she couldn't blame the concussion for her sudden light-headedness. "You should leave the investigating to the police. Especially now with the accident."

Belinda's eyes opened wide. "Do you think—?"

"I do. Parker will find who did this. But you need to lie low."

Belinda's heart might have slowed up but her mind still worked. She glanced sideways. "Aren't you going to ask me what I was doing there?"

Bennett's cool eyes warmed up again. "Is that the right question?"

Belinda didn't expect that response. "What question would you like me to ask?"

"I'm more curious about the 'why' momentarily."

Belinda stuck her thumbs in and out of her back pockets, debating if she dared tell him. It was all itching inside of her and here was a perfectly willing listener who might know something she did not. Not that he would be as willing to share. Still, it was awfully tempting.

"You see," she said, leaning into one hip, "Lily was at the party, which is very strange considering she hasn't been around in, oh, about ten years. Do you know about Mark?"

Bennett nodded.

"Okay, well, backtracking a little to not too long after that happened, Lily left to go to school out of state and she just sort of fell off the radar. The accident shook everyone up and most of us drifted apart not long afterward. In any case, it was clear at the funeral that whatever connection she had to Stellan, Jeff, and the others was done for."

"How do you know?" His gray eyes had grown more intense as she spoke. Good. She had his attention.

"It's not like she stood up and announced that she would have nothing to do with them anymore, but I saw her and Jeff in some sort of intense discussion after the funeral, apart from everyone. I don't know what they said to each other, but neither of them was happy. But they were unhappy in different ways. Does that make sense?"

"Not at all."

"How about this: Jeff looked despondent and Lily looked angry."

"Better."

Belinda inhaled. "I think Jeff was just seeking forgiveness, but I don't think that was the right time to do it."

"Would it have been the right time at the party?"

Now he had her attention. Belinda tried not to seem too eager for information. "It has been a long time since Mark died. On the other hand, death is a powerful cloud." Belinda didn't want to ask what he knew directly so tossed out some bait instead. "I may have seen Jeff and Lily having a similar conversation at the party to the one I witnessed at Mark's funeral."

"Outside?"

Belinda's eyes lit up. "On the gazebo." Oh, forget it. She stunk at taking back doors. "Did you see them? It was dark so I can't be certain."

Bennett frowned. "I didn't have cameras or people on that part of the lawn." His hands dropped to his sides. "But we did see them leave the house together at one point."

"Oh." Belinda looked disappointed. "Why not?"

"Stellan didn't hire us for perimeter security. Only indoors, mostly to protect the bedrooms."

"Which were all locked." Belinda folded her arms across her chest.

"You would know. You tested them all."

Belinda narrowed her eyes. "I was looking for the stupid bathroom! It's not my fault Stellan's house is a labyrinth." She tapped her foot. "You know the fact that Stellan didn't have...perimeter security?"

Bennett nodded approval. "That's either unfortunate or very convenient."

"I think it's both," Bennett said, holding up the leaf again. He was not going to let that go, was he? "Now what were you doing snooping in Lily Devore's house?"

Belinda screwed up her face in indignation. "I was not snooping in anyone's house! Do I look like the sort that waltzes into people's homes and rifles through their stuff?"

"Yes."

Belinda huffed. "Thank you for taking a moment to think about your answer."

"It's a simple deduction. You eavesdrop and you lie about your identity. Why shouldn't you snoop?"

"I..." Belinda felt the feistiness fizzle out of her, but straightened her back anyway. "You don't even know me."

His lip did that thing again where it curled up ever so slightly. "What did you find?"

"Nothing...I didn't have time." Belinda looked up at him through her eyelashes. "Don't you believe me?"

"You were distracted, frazzled I would say, by something you found in that house. You did not look like that because you almost got caught."

Of course he was right, but it was still irritating that he could figure all of that out just by looking at her. Belinda hesitated. "Just some old photographs. Of Mark."

Bennett's eyes probed hers and she fought the urge to look away.

Bennett accepted that. Not that he believed that was the whole story, but he would respect her refusal to divulge everything.

"There might be something else," Belinda said, her escape down the Ocean Walk reminding her of something. "There is a back way up to the Mayhew's home that bypasses the front gate. It's not obvious, but we

Cliffhanger

used to go that way as kids. Do you think the police already know about it?"

Bennett pulled out his phone to find out. She could hear Jonas' muted replies from where she stood and he sounded eager for Belinda to show them as soon as possible. While Bennett wrapped up their conversation, her second visitor in a day rounded the corner of the house.

Jarrett held a balloon with "Get Well Soon!" and a rainbow across the front in one hand, and a bouquet of miscellaneous flowers in the other. Belinda felt bad for tricking him at the market like that, but it might look like she hadn't right now anyway. His face lit up at seeing her.

As soon as he saw Bennett, however, his happiness balloon popped.

Nervous now, Belinda introduced him to Bennett. He shook Bennett's hand, his blue eyes iced over. How awkward was this? Belinda wanted to say something to make Jarrett feel better, but she was starting to feel dizzy. And, well, faint.

Bennett caught her before she tumbled to the porch floor. Jarrett ran to her as Bennett scooped her up and carried her to the closest soft surface—the couch in the living room, visible through the window. Bennett cupped her cheek with his palm as Belinda's eyes flickered.

"She'll be okay," Bennett said. "I think you should go home now."

Jarrett stuck to his place at Belinda's head. "Maybe you should go home."

Bennett just stared at him. "Come back to visit tomorrow. She'll be up for company then."

"What about you? You're company."

"Right now I'm help until her brother gets home."

Jarrett's lips formed a hard line as he held Bennett's gaze. "The flowers need water."

"I'll find a vase."

Jarrett pushed himself up off the floor and stomped out as Belinda came to.

Belinda blinked to life, her eyes foggy. "Oh," she said weakly. "Are you ready to go see the path now?"

Bennett suppressed his desire to laugh. "Maybe tomorrow. But you're not going anywhere just yet."

Admittedly relieved, Belinda rested her head on the pillow, Bennett's gray eyes the last thing she saw for a while as she dropped off to sleep.

~ * ~

Belinda narrowly got out the door the next night without telling Kyle about the path to Stellan's. Bennett had walked halfway to the front door when she popped out and jogged toward his truck. Well, jogged was exaggerating. She moved faster than a snail's pace. A really slow snail's pace.

"You didn't have to get out," she said, peeking behind her and hauling herself up into his black SUV. She could see Kyle poking his head around the blinds in the front windows, but had to close her eyes to let the dizziness settle.

Bennett casually got back in and followed her line of sight. "Is he going to follow us?"

Belinda laughed. Bennett's lips curled up, pleased that he elicited that reaction. "He can just be a little protective." And she was evasive and he's suspicious, Belinda thought.

Jonas beat them to the turnaround where Belinda had parked in the past, leaning up against a gray sedan and playing with his smartphone.

He nodded to Bennett, smiling widely as Belinda stepped out of the passenger's side. "You've been kidnapped," he said, shaking her hand. Belinda looked at the path encased in shadow and lit only by a partial moon.

"Could the person have had a flashlight?" she said dubiously.

Jonas grinned, waving a flashlight to and fro. "Bennett will go with you, honey."

That placated her, so she took to the slope.

Belinda took the lead, self-conscious with Bennett walking behind her. She hoped her clothes behaved and that the jeans she wore actually flattered her butt. And why was she worried about him staring at her butt anyway? Oh, no. What if he was staring at her butt? Belinda tugged at the hem of her shirt, trying to will it lower.

They were on an uphill climb that wound from the turnaround to the Mayhew property. Wild flowers and sea grasses made it look like it led nowhere. But it was a good workout for your thighs and a bit difficult to navigate in ballet flats. There were no lights on that side of the property and a few trees nearby let you safely bob from the wild grasses to the trunks without having to step out into the open.

She found it actually wasn't as dark as it seemed at the bottom. Enough of the moonlight reflected off of the water, shooting a decent glow in front of her feet. They made it to the top of the property and stood toward the cliff.

"What if Jeff was just standing there, thinking or something?" Belinda looked out at the cliff's edge soberly. "He could have been lost in thought and not even realized someone had come up this side of the property. With the waves, his own distraction, it would have been all too easy to just push him off." She demonstrated, throwing her arms out in front of her. "You were right about no one noticing from inside either." She pointed to where the party had taken place. "It's too far out. And that music was insanely loud."

"Everything all right up there?" Jonas said through the walkie-talkie he gave her.

Belinda searched for the right button to push, turning it to different angles to make it out in the light. Bennett slipped it from her palm, holding it to his mouth. "We're fine. It was no problem getting up here."

"Excellent. You can come down then before someone thinks you're trying to break in."

Bennett rolled his eyes and stuffed the walkie-talkie in his jacket pocket, pulling out a mini flashlight. He flicked it on, shining it ahead of them.

"You come prepared, don't you?" The light reflected off of something and Belinda started to reach out to grab Bennett's arm when the world started to spin. She hit a pebble that started a landslide that sent her feet up and the rest of her down. She hit bottom with a grunt and Bennett whirled around to help her, whistling for Jonas.

"You have a whistle signal too?" she said, trying to sit up. Her hands stung from the fall and when she held them up to brush them off, she thought she saw blood. Jonas and his flashlight appeared on the hill, and he crouched over her, worry crinkling the skin around his eyes.

"I saw something reflect in the light," she said, deciding she needed a moment before standing again.

Bennett picked Belinda up by her waist and scooted her over a foot so they could look where her palm had hit dirt. Buried in with the gravel was an earring. Jonas whipped out a pair of tweezers and held it up in the light. It was a silver stud.

"Rather plain." Belinda frowned. "I don't think this came from any woman that Stellan invited."

"Maybe it doesn't belong to a woman." Bennett met her eyes and lifted his brows in significance while Jonas dropped it in a plastic baggie. Then Bennett held Belinda by the waist and carefully led her back down.

If she hadn't felt so discombobulated and heavy and just relieved to have him keeping her upright, Belinda would have had chill bumps from his taut arm flexing against her back and the way his finger grazed her skin where her shirt had lifted up. But all she could think about was sitting back down.

"Battle scars." Jonas winked at Belinda as she swung her legs out of the truck while Bennett pulled items out of his first aid kit. "This is a huge help. It could turn things around."

"I should have told you earlier."

Jonas shrugged it off. "Out of sight, out of mind sort of thing. Doesn't matter. We know now."

Belinda didn't feel quite so nonchalant about it. Something about the whole situation made her wonder if she'd made a mistake telling them.

Bennett cleaned off her hands, Belinda wincing as he squirted disinfectant onto the cuts. She looked up at the Mayhew property while he added the finishing touches of bandages to her palms.

Jonas smiled. "It's hard to leave a job unfinished, isn't it?" His face turned darker as he checked a message on his phone. He forced one last grin for Belinda and saluted both of them and drove off, probably headed back to the station for a long night. Belinda realized it was the first time she'd witnessed him drive away instead of peddle.

Bennett took his time repackaging the first aid kit, so she waited patiently with her hands folded in her lap. He finally snapped the top of it shut and came around to her door, moonlight creating silvery highlights in his dark hair. "Would you like to go get a coffee?"

Belinda smiled, her cheeks finally flushing pink for the right reasons. "Coffee's always welcome."

Instead of being holed up in the coffee shop with the three other people hanging out, they got their beverages to go and strolled through downtown, passing dormant shops waiting for summer. Most of the small boutiques hadn't opened for the season yet, but there was the sense of anticipation on the streets in the daytime. Stray tourists had already begun to slip in and Belinda shivered with excitement. It would be her first summer in Portside in two years and she couldn't wait for the beaching, the shopping, and the people swarming the town.

"All the shops will open soon," she said, watching her step on the cobblestone street, gravitating toward the shop windows. One day in the not-too-distant future, one of those would belong to her.

"Do you plan to shop 'til you drop?"

Belinda laughed. The second time in a row. Bennett was on a roll.

"Not yet, though I do have a wedding shower present to buy." She perused the window display of one of the shops. "I hate all this sort of stuff. They have all kinds of useless or expensive items on their gift registry that I don't want to buy. On the other hand, it will be much easier just to pick one of those than to come up with something original that they may or may not like."

"You could always go green. Everybody likes that."

Belinda smirked. "I am not giving those people money. A gift is one thing, but neither of them need the cash, believe me."

"So we're talking a society wedding?"

"My aunt and her husband are paying for the wedding, custom-designed dresses and all, and I believe that the groom's parents are giving them a lavish honeymoon as a gift. I'm pretty sure I heard Bali mentioned at one of my fittings."

"Fittings?"

"I am one of the privileged seven who gets to walk down the aisle in a custom-designed bridesmaid's gown. It means I have to abstain from food until after their June wedding."

Bennett lifted his eyebrows.

"And that brings me back to your original question," Belinda went on. "Instead of shopping, I plan to eat gelato and sugar cookies until I can't stand the sight of them."

"They don't have gelato or sugar cookies where you've been?"

"Not like here." She skipped over a dip in the rocks. "I have to admit, it's mostly the warm, fuzzy memories of going there with my family and friends."

"I wasn't sure if you had any of those from Portside."

Belinda glanced at him curiously. "I have plenty of good memories. There are dark moments too." Her eyes wandered away. "Really dark moments."

"I'm sorry. I didn't mean to—"

Belinda shook her head. She wasn't letting that shadow settle upon her at that moment. "Don't be. It happened. We all tried to hide from it, but we can't anymore." She sighed heavily. "I've always felt more for Kyle than myself, but..."

Bennett held his breath.

"I lost Mark too." She kept her eyes on the cobblestones.

Bennett waited a minute for her to elucidate, but it seemed that was all she would say on that subject. "Are you sorry you came back now?"

Belinda smiled. "You don't mess around, do you?"

Bennett's brow creased. "What do you mean?"

Belinda laughed again, but this time Bennett had no idea why. "I'm sorry...I don't mean to laugh. It's just...you really don't know?"

"I know I'm straightforward." His jaw tightened up. "Does that bother you?"

Belinda left him in suspense, choosing to take a minute to think it over. "Not at all. I rather like it."

Bennett nodded. "Good."

"And I'm not sorry I came back to Portside. I'm not sorry at all." Bennett looked pleased with her response. "So now I'm going to turn the tables and be straightforward with you. How long have you and the detective been friends?"

"Too long." Belinda laughed again and Bennett suppressed a smile. "We met at the Academy and led parallel lives for a while, working in the same station, moving in the same direction. We even did some private investigating work together on the side."

"Bennett Tate, PI." Belinda's eyes sparkled. "It sounds good together."

"It's not as thrilling as you'd think."

"What? No high-speed car chases or dramatic slow-walks away from exploding buildings?" Belinda turned thoughtful. "I bet you were good."

Bennett hesitated. "I did all right."

"No, no. I'm confident it suited you."

"How would you know?" As with everything he asked, he said it with perfect seriousness. He sincerely wanted to know how she came to that conclusion.

"Easy. You don't miss a thing. In fact, I believe I heard someone call you the gray-eyed eagle."

Bennett raised his eyebrows, surprised and delighted that she knew his eye color. "May I ask who that someone was?"

"Me." Belinda grinned mischievously. "Of course, I'm not sure I intended it as a compliment at the time."

"Was it when you wanted to...hire me...for Victoria's party?"

"I think so."

"Then I'm sure it wasn't."

Belinda giggled. "Well, I've changed my mind. It's now officially a compliment." Belinda now admired, even liked, his keen eyes. And she was glad he'd brushed by her in the hallway at Stellan's and saved her from Jarrett at the market and then again near the cemetery. Someday, she would ask him about all of these coincidental meetings, but for that night, Belinda was just happy they'd met.

"I'll add it to my business card."

"It could be your new slogan: 'Stay safe with the gray-eyed eagle.'"

"New? It would be the first."

"You don't have one?" Belinda screwed up her nose, trying to remember what was on his website. "No, you don't. That's a shame."

"Well, I promise to get your input if I decide to change that."

"Please do. I'd love to help." Their eyes met, Belinda's sparkly and Bennett's warm like the fur of those funny dogs she still couldn't remember the name of. And there was nothing in the past or present that could dampen the anticipation burning in her chest.

Chapter 10

Bennett returned her back to her house reluctantly, and Belinda floated back to the kitchen, mulling over possible slogans for Bennett's business and dreaming about pumpkin pie for some reason, deciding that she'd have to add a pumpkin pie cupcake to her menu.

"Hey, Bels," Kyle said, sitting on the couch in the living room in the dark. Belinda walked toward him, all the shimmer in her diminishing as he glanced at her sideways. "Have fun with your new friend?"

Belinda assessed the situation. She nodded, deciding less was more at that moment.

"You showed them the path, huh? The path that takes you onto the Mayhew property, bypassing the gate?"

"It could be important."

Kyle stared straight ahead. "Then there's something I should tell you now because it may come out anyway."

Belinda straightened up, her heart flip-flopping.

"I was there the night of the party," he said, avoiding her eyes. "To talk to Jeff."

Belinda stared at him in disbelief. "But...but you haven't spoken to him in years!"

"I wanted to make things right between us. It was time."

"Time?" It crossed her mind that under other circumstances this would have come as great news. Right now, it was just a huge mess. "You were mad at me for going to the party in the first place. For risking seeing Jeff. Now you're telling me you wanted to make things right between the two of you?"

Cliffhanger

"That was you, this is me. I would never trust him with you, but I needed to say a few things to him."

"Like what?"

"That's not really any of your business."

Belinda crossed her arms over her chest. Kyle brought this up, volunteered actually, and now it was none of her business. "Uh...okay. So did you talk to Jeff?"

"Yeah, I did." Kyle's eyes were distant. "I snuck up that path and found him alone in the yard. We talked and I left the way I came."

"And that was it? You just had a casual chat with a person you wouldn't deal with for the past ten years and went home to watch TV?"

Kyle's eyes flashed. "What do you think I did? Push him over the cliff?"

"No! But I can't believe it was that normal either." Why did he opt to tell her this at all if he was going to tell half-truths?

Kyle sighed. "He was shocked to see me, but glad I think. We both avoided mentioning you and we made our peace and I went home, leaving him alone—and alive—in the backyard."

"Are you sure you were alone?"

"Yes. I wouldn't have talked to him otherwise."

"And all you did was...make peace? You didn't talk about anything else?" Belinda could feel the irritation emanating off of Kyle, but again, he brought it up. If he didn't want to divulge anything, he should have kept it to himself.

"It was a brief conversation."

"And you are absolutely positive no one saw you?"

Kyle glanced at her curiously. "Why are you so adamant about that?"

Belinda dropped her hands to her sides. "The killer could have used that path. I was just thinking that someone might have noticed you coming or going that way and gotten an idea of how to avoid being seen.

They could have officially left the party and then returned that way to kill Jeff. And that would have been good timing if he was alone when you left."

"Will you tell your friend about this?"

Belinda examined his profile. She didn't want to have to do anything, but he didn't seem to be leaving her with much choice. "I really think you should just go tell the police yourself. It could save you a lot of trouble later. If you don't, it just looks like you're hiding something." As she said it, Belinda bit her lip. It didn't *look* like he was hiding something, he *was* hiding something.

Kyle swallowed. "I'm sorry, Bels. I'm really sorry." He kissed her forehead and headed to his room.

"Does that mean you won't?" Belinda's voice echoed along with her frustration.

He didn't answer, leaving her alone in what now felt like a big, empty box. Belinda took a deep breath, trying to steady her nerves. Why was every pleasant moment in her life scarred like this? She would wait and try and talk some sense into him in the morning. If he still refused...well, she would try not to think about that.

Kyle avoided her in the morning, barricading himself in his bedroom. Belinda sat at the kitchen island trying to work on her to-do list for her cupcake boutique, thoughts of Kyle "making peace'" with Jeff and Bennett's gray eyes absorbing her concentration. So when the doorbell rang, Belinda wasn't at all prepared to deal with anyone.

Bennett's detective friend was outside her door with a uniformed officer behind him. Belinda's eyes shot open and all other thoughts evaporated.

"Is your brother around this morning, Ms. Kittridge?" he said.

So they were back to that. Last night, he'd called her honey, which Belinda could only guess meant something incredibly awful was

Cliffhanger

about to happen. Belinda nodded and stepped aside for them to enter and then flew up the stairs to Kyle's room, banging on his door. He opened, glowering, until he saw the detective.

"Mr. Kittridge," Jonas said in his official voice, "you're under arrest for the murder of Jeff Clark."

Kyle ignored the involuntary squeak that shot out of Belinda's mouth and let them handcuff him and lead him outside without a word, refusing to even glance in Belinda's direction. She followed them out, staring blankly as the officer helped him into the back of the police car.

Belinda could only watch from a distance, feeling more helpless than she ever had, and she'd felt pretty helpless in the past.

"Do you have anyone you can call?" Jonas said with a less official tone.

"Our parents are on a cruise."

He nodded in understanding. "Will you be okay?"

"I...I think. I'm not the type to go into hysterics if that's what you mean."

Jonas smiled. "I didn't believe so." He dug his hands in his pockets, staring at the grass. "This is entirely off record of course, but I would call Bennett if I were you." Jonas nodded to her, slipped into the passenger's side of one of the patrol cars, and ambled away. Once they were out of earshot, she could only hear the distant whining of a landscaping tool and her own heartbeat.

Before she'd opened the door to the police, Belinda had felt hurt, but now she was on the verge of a complete meltdown. Kyle had shut the door in her face, refusing to open up and tell her exactly what happened. And now this. And their parents were out of the country. Belinda had just told the detective she wouldn't go into hysterics. Well, maybe she'd lied.

Belinda stood there in a daze for a few minutes, thinking numbly whether she was actually in a dream. Deciding that was a lost cause, she plodded back into the house and up the stairs, her steps seeming to echo louder than before, and flipped open her computer. She typed in Tate Security and called Bennett.

He made it to her house in insanely good time, less put together than she was used to. His short hair spiked out in all directions, and he'd buttoned his shirt wrong. Still in a daze, Belinda automatically started to fix it for him.

"Jonas suggested I call you," she said, struggling with the last button. Bennett waited patiently as she forced it through the slot, maybe too surprised to offer to help.

She flattened out his shirt panel so the buttons aligned properly, his skin peeking out through the gap, and patted down the material gently. As she started buttoning it back, Belinda realized what on earth she was doing and got nervous, fumbling with her task. Bennett took her hands, now shaking, and walked her over to the kitchen island, helping her onto a stool.

"It's harder from the outside," she mumbled, trying to relax.

Bennett finished buttoning his shirt. "Do you have a lawyer you can call?"

"Yes."

"Well, you should." Bennett frowned. "I know some of what's going on here and it's not in your brother's favor. They found evidence that he'd been on the cliff. Paint particles I think. And they believe Kyle and Jeff got into a fight."

Belinda wrung her hands. "The scratch on his arm..."

"Yeah." Bennett's mouth gaped like he was about to say something else but changed his mind.

"What?"

"The car that rammed you was a rental."

"So, in other words, it doesn't help?"

"No, they found out who it was rented to." Bennett averted his eyes.

"Who?" Belinda said suspiciously. She had a feeling she wasn't going to like his answer.

"Your brother."

Belinda shook trying to squash down the rage in her chest. "No."

She was barely audible, but from the redness in her face to her stiff upper body, Bennett had gotten the response he anticipated.

Belinda walked around the kitchen island, randomly opening up kitchen cabinets, which were all empty. Her hands shook while she poured water into a glass and her cheeks tightened. She was about to cry, wasn't she?

After barely managing to gulp down one drink of water, it started. Belinda was obviously trying hard not to lose it, but she was also obviously losing the battle. Before he could think of what to do, she ran from the room and up the nearby staircase. He heard a door slam and then...nothing. Bennett stood in the kitchen, torn on what to do.

After going back and forth, he decided to wait downstairs. He didn't want to leave her like that, not with her brother under arrest. So he sat down at their kitchen island and opened the notebook sitting there, figuring he could make a list of things he needed from the hardware store while he waited. He flipped for a blank page, passing a random scribble dead in the center of the notebook. Out of curiosity, he flipped back to see what it said. Someone had slashed an address diagonally across the page. Bennett flipped back to the beginning. Random lists and notes covered the pages. The handwriting did not match that of the address.

A door creaked and then Bennett heard soft padding on the wood floor upstairs. He closed the notebook and pushed it back into place where he'd found it, repeating the address to himself. Belinda appeared at the bottom of the stairs, disappeared as she hit the landing, and reappeared a second later at the edge of the kitchen. She looked paler than when he arrived and now her brown eyes were bloodshot. They also looked surprised to see him.

Belinda tugged on the ends of her sleeves and hugged her body, avoiding his eyes. "I figured you'd left," she said quietly, but not with the ferocity of her earlier statement. She cleared her throat and poured more water, gulping without a problem this time.

Bennett hoped he hadn't messed up by not leaving, but it was too late. He couldn't think of a question that didn't sound lame, so he stayed quiet, letting her pad around and drink more water and search through the cabinets. She found cookies and nestled into a seat next to him, setting the package between the two of them and offering him one.

"You first," he said, his voice echoing in the house like it was built of marble.

She nibbled on the edge of the cookie. "I'm sorry. I'm not good at public hysterics."

"Neither am I."

Belinda's face started to come back to life. "You can ask me now," she said.

"Ask you what?"

"Whatever you wanted to before I went nutty."

Bennett raised his eyebrows, taking a minute to remember. "Why did your brother want to talk to Clark?"

"To make peace." She exaggerated her words.

"You don't believe him?"

Belinda scrunched her nose. "Not really...but I don't think he killed Jeff either. Or rammed into me."

Bennett nodded. "Someone saw your brother exchange heated words with Jeff the other day outside of one of the cemeteries. And apparently that wasn't the first time that had happened."

"It was probably where Mark is buried. Do you know what they were arguing about?"

Bennett shrugged. "Maybe Kyle was concerned that Jeff would pick up where he left off obsessing over you."

"As flattering as that is I don't think it was Kyle's top priority."

Bennett leaned closer to her. "Did you know Mark well?"

Belinda felt her body tense and her mind drifted off to that final summer when Mark died.... "Oh...um, well enough, but he was primarily Kyle's friend." She avoided his eyes and focused on her cookie.

"Was he a good sailor?"

"Oh, yeah." Belinda waved her hand like everyone should know that. "He rivaled Kyle, and that's saying something."

"So he should have known what he was doing."

Belinda didn't know where this random line of thinking was heading, but she shrugged and answered anyway. "Beyond. He actually taught lessons at the yacht club in the summer." Belinda watched Bennett's eyes, deep in puzzle solving. "Are you thinking...are you thinking Mark's accident wasn't an accident?" Her throat constricted saying the words.

Bennett looked at her questioningly. "Is that what you're thinking right now?"

"I don't know, but I'm thinking about how good a sailor Mark was and that conversation between Jeff and Stellan at the party..." She pursed her lips. "It could explain some things."

"Such as?"

"Their behavior afterward. Jeff was a train wreck right from the beginning, but Stellan was totally reserved about the whole thing. I just wanted to know what happened, but he was very vague on some points and always got defensive. Maybe...maybe that's because they weren't telling the whole truth." She'd always had that feeling whenever she talked to Stellan.

"I think it's worth considering with everything that's happened. It could be you've accidentally started to unearth something you shouldn't know."

Belinda yawned and Bennett took that as his cue to let her rest for a while. She'd had a lot going on. Belinda snatched the edge of his sleeve as he stepped out onto the stoop. Belinda's eyes were still dim, but her face looked a little less pale than it had when he got there.

"Are we okay?" Belinda said timidly. She was scared. More scared than she wanted to admit, and the house started to collapse in on her as Bennett walked out the door. Without Kyle around, she was completely alone.

Bennett held her arms, stepping close so she inhaled that spicy scent always lingering on his skin like he'd walked through a bazaar in some exotic location. "I can't make promises, Belinda. But I will do everything in my power to help you and keep you safe."

His eyes had tightened and grown that darker shade of gray they did when Bennett flipped into serious mode. Just knowing that he was so serious about what was going on made Belinda feel calmer as she strolled back into the kitchen after he left, not in a huge hurry to do anything. *Great*, she thought, staring at the kitchen floor. Right by the side door was a mud smear that Kyle had conveniently ignored. Belinda sighed and bent down to wipe it up with a wet paper towel when it hit her that the smudge was not there that morning. And Kyle wasn't home yet, and Bennett came through the front.

Belinda sucked in a shallow breath. While she had been languishing upstairs, thinking she was all alone, someone else had been right there with her.

Chapter 11

Maybe the mud smear was nothing. Maybe she was just paranoid now, Belinda thought as she opened her eyes. The next day brought rain showers, the first unpleasant weather in weeks to Belinda's recollection. She felt relieved looking out the window that morning though and seeing something drearier than perfect sun. It was more fitted to the actual circumstances.

Before the revelation that Mark's death might have been more than an accident, Belinda was just confused. Confused by Kyle's behavior and actions and the evidence surrounding Jeff's murder. Now the pieces were coming together like bits of glass in a mosaic. It wasn't rounded off at the edges. No, it was sharp and jagged. But it was getting clearer.

Victoria had insisted she stay over the night before and as she followed the smell of something delicious to the kitchen, Belinda was glad she'd taken her up on it, even if it was a pain to pack up all of her stuff. Why did you need so much for only one night anyway? But it beat being alone in that big house.

Egg batter splashed out as Victoria threw pieces of bread slathered in it on the griddle. Belinda poured some coffee, yawning as she dumped spoonfuls of sugar into the cup. Victoria grinned. "It looks like you need that."

"I may drink the whole pot, just to warn you." Belinda watched her flip the egg-enveloped pieces of bread with longing. "I heart French toast."

"That's why I made it." Victoria set the spatula down on the granite countertop. "Do you think Bennett fancies French toast? Maybe I should call him and invite him over for breakfast."

Belinda narrowed her eyes. "Do you see what I look like right now? Don't even tease me about it."

"Something tells me he'd be just as happy to see you."

Belinda self-consciously stuffed a stray lock behind her ear as if Bennett would magically appear in the room.

They each filled a plate and sat down at the pedestal table. "So you still haven't filled me in about your recent escapades," Victoria said, shimmying in her seat to get comfortable.

"I think 'escapades' is blowing things out of proportion."

"I don't know. You're running up and down the coast with a pretty hot guy. I'd call that an escapade personally."

Belinda took her time chewing the first bite. "Let's see. We met his detective friend at the base of that hill you can climb up to reach the Mayhew house."

"Ah, yes. The backdoors to everyone's property that we all used to be so familiar with."

"So I led them up and had a complete panic attack imagining Bennett staring at my derriere."

Victoria raised one perfectly plucked eyebrow. Belinda seriously needed to find out what salon she went to. "I'm sure he was but you have nothing to worry about. Trust me. I'm sure he enjoyed the view." Victoria winked.

"Then I made a complete fool of myself and crashed on the way down, but we found an earring stud on the path, which could be useful. At least, I'm positive that piece of evidence won't point at Kyle." Belinda wiped syrup from her lips. "Once Bennett took care of my newly acquired cuts, he asked if I wanted to go get a coffee, so we did and then we spent a while walking through downtown."

Victoria's eyes sparkled. "You didn't tell me that!"

"I was saving it." Belinda grinned.

"You minx. What did you talk about?" Victoria pulled her chair in closer, practically leaning her entire body across the table.

"Oh, this and that. He doesn't have a slogan for his business so I teased him that it should be 'stay safe with the gray-eyed eagle' or something like that."

"Watch. It'll be on his website soon."

Belinda laughed. "I doubt it, but I have been trying to think of a suitable catchphrase for him."

"So this talking with each other stuff will keep happening I take it."

Belinda glanced heavenward. "At least right now. He seems to want to help, especially with Kyle and all."

"Hmm...I wonder why? Oh, that's right. It's because of you."

"He told me he likes the puzzle."

"And you."

"He likes putting it all together."

"And you."

"Then there's no doubt the satisfaction of seeing justice meted out."

"And you."

Belinda aimed her fork at Victoria's head then stabbed another piece of sausage. "And me, naturally. I am his French toast."

"Now that should be on his website."

"Along with a photo of what he looked like yesterday morning." A smile crept onto Belinda's face just remembering it. Every time she saw him, Bennett looked more handsome to her.

"Ooh...was he all morning sexy?"

"He was more like just got out of bed sexy." She tried to demonstrate what his hair looked like with her hands.

"But he was sexy."

"Yeah." Belinda sighed and bit into another piece. "That seems to be one of his bad habits. That and getting way to close to me for the good of either of us."

"Indeed. You sound incredibly disturbed. Maybe you should tell him to just back off already." Victoria waved her coffee cup around, almost spilling it all over her floor.

"I would except I like it too much. And it's hard not to like a guy who doesn't run away from you when you're having a complete meltdown." Belinda drew an invisible swirl on the tabletop. She felt guilty for being anywhere near happy with everything going on though. And for being relieved that she didn't have to worry about bumping into Jeff again. And scared for Kyle...and herself.

"I hate to abandon you like this." Victoria dabbed at the corners of her mouth with a napkin. "Especially when our conversation revolves around a sexy man, but I have the future of piano concerts sitting on my shoulders."

"I forgot you have the spring recital coming up soon."

"Yes, and one of my students has some family stuff going on right now and is behind, so we have an extra long session scheduled today so I can help her catch up. Frankly, I need to practice myself." Victoria stood, smiling. "But you just sit tight and drink all the coffee you want. I will be stranded over at that black monstrosity in the corner for the better part of the morning." Victoria pointed at the upright piano in the living room.

Belinda sipped her coffee, listening to Victoria drill out snippets of what she thought could be Mozart. Then Victoria packed up her gear and Dan picked her up and hauled her off to the music school where she now taught advanced students—and had learned once herself.

Without the music and the distraction of another person in the house, Belinda's mind wandered to Kyle's predicament and the dark cloud that his name was on the rental that hit her and Victoria. But she didn't have long to wallow as Jarrett had managed to find out where Belinda had gone.

He brought another balloon and fresh flowers and was delighted to see no one else was there. He dumped his backpack beside the couch and after asking her several times how she was feeling, leaned forward on his knees with his hands clasped like he was about to say something important. Belinda wanted to sigh. *Not now, Jarrett. Please.*

"Is that guy your boyfriend?" Jarrett said.

Belinda had tried to sit up nice and proper, but couldn't stand it for long, so just sunk into the cushions. Jarrett's feelings about Bennett were not high on her priority list right then. "He's a friend, Jarrett."

"You were holding hands at the store."

"Friends hold hands sometimes." This was all getting way too complicated for her.

"We've never held hands," he said quietly, focused on his own, spindly and tan.

Maybe she should explain. Maybe. But Jarrett's back and forth niceness didn't encourage her to come out with the truth. He needed to let this whole idea go. The sooner, the better.

She didn't answer and after a minute, he sat up straighter and asked to use the bathroom. Jarrett's backpack tipped over after he left and Belinda bent to put it back in place when she saw something peeking out. She unzipped the front pocket and pulled out a huge wad of cold, hard cash.

The upstairs door shut and Belinda dropped the cash back in the pocket and zipped it up just in time for Jarrett to tromp down the stairs. She smiled as he came over and lifted up his pack.

"Guess I should get going," he said curtly. Belinda started to get up, but he held out his hand. "Don't bother." Without a good-bye, Jarrett threw open the front door and left, but not before Belinda took note of the mud and grass caked onto the side of his sneakers.

She chewed on her bottom lip, originally planning to stay home all day. But now Belinda doubted she could stand it. There was too much to think about, and now the house seemed to compress her thoughts even more. It was time to get some fresh air.

~ * ~

Bennett picked up a whole quahog shell at the edge of the tide, tipping out the water that had collected inside. At some point, this had been home to a strange, alien-like creature. Now, it was probably in the stomach of one of the seagulls squatting on the beach.

He flipped the shell over, running his thumb along the ridges. He wasn't one for collections, though he did have a few shells he'd picked up over the years sitting around the house. But he didn't know how to display them, at least well. Belinda might know more about that, if their house was any indication.

Not that he should be feeding into his growing attraction to her. It wasn't the same situation; it wasn't. But it was close. A girl from a wealthy Portside family wrapped up in a scandal. And the previous one had worn all the same signs of interest. Bennett smirked. Jonas would shoot that remark down without blinking. In fact, he might bring it up next time just to see what he said. But, objectively, Bennett had to counter that thought too. In hindsight, there had been red alerts before from the beginning, but he didn't know enough to recognize them. Maybe he didn't know enough to recognize them now either, but he would try.

"Bennett!"

Bennett's head shot up in the direction of the strained feminine voice. Belinda waved, jogging in his direction. He practically dropped the

Cliffhanger

quahog on his foot. Had he wished her there somehow? She smiled and he could picture her eyes sparkling underneath the sunglasses. She had her jeans rolled up and looked like she'd come there on her way from somewhere else while Bennett had his running gear on. Now that he'd stopped for a few minutes, he could feel the sweat coagulating on his back. Great.

"Are you shell gathering?" she said, kicking up damp sand as she walked.

Bennett looked at her quizzically until she pointed at the shell now hanging limply in his hand. "I like shells." *Oh, boy,* he thought. Here we go again, sounding like an idiot. Not being prepared for conversation never worked in his favor and he could feel color rising in his neck. "I mean, photographing them. Because of the detail. Though I collect them too."

Now she looked at him quizzically. Or that's what he interpreted from her mouth. "You photograph too?" She took a step closer, reaching her hand out for the shell.

Of all the thousands of things shooting like stars through his mind at that moment, the joy that she stepped closer to him and how near her hand was to his was instantly replaced with horror that he must smell awful. If she noticed, it didn't register on her face.

"So, you mean, you do more than just snap off-center photos with your phone like me?" Belinda grinned, pleased with her self-deprecating humor.

Bennett temporarily forgot that he smelled and with absolutely no red alerts blaring, he flipped the shell over and showed her the ridges. "I was thinking of trying out some close-ups of the ridges. I've been doing other things lately, but it would be a good texture to work with and would give me a new project."

"What other things?" Belinda lit up.

"Water, actually. I have more shots than I can count of spray on the Ocean Walk."

"So you do frequent the Walk. I thought as much."

Bennett's heart raced a little faster. Did that mean she thought about him when they weren't together too?

She sounded much more down to earth than she had during their last conversation, and Belinda explained that she'd stayed with Victoria the night before, which relieved Bennett. Apparently her friend's hospitality had calmed her down. Staying in a house with other people helped and, according to Belinda, the French toast and sausage from that morning's breakfast made a big difference in her outlook.

Bennett's mouth crooked up as Belinda recounted these thoughts in a manner that reminded him of an underwater current. Fast, unyielding, and inescapable. She pulled him in and carried him off to sea before he knew he couldn't see land anymore. It was incredible. And what was worse, Bennett didn't mind. At all.

But something in her manner was still off. It was probably her brother, but still...

"Are you out for a walk?" Bennett looked her over again. Not that he needed to, but he couldn't stop himself.

"I thought a walk might help me get some things straight in my head."

Something was bothering her. He thought so, even if she did ramble on happily about Victoria's breakfast. "Is it working?"

Belinda tugged on the ends of the ties on her hoodie. "Yes and no. Right now, I'm all brain-cloudy."

"Can I help?"

Belinda looked sad. "The car that hit us is really bothering me. Kyle doesn't need to tell me he didn't have anything to do with it, but..." She just trailed off, caressing the edge of the shell he still held. Bennett couldn't pin down why, but he felt she was holding something back from him.

"But why is his name on the rental?" Bennett offered. Belinda nodded weakly. "Jonas will figure it out. He's fair and he's never happy with the obvious solution. It'll be okay." It sounded like a pathetic condolence considering everything her brother was facing. His entire future hung on this evidence.

But the little assurance he could offer seemed to lighten her up and Belinda gave him a lopsided smile. She took a deep breath. "You're right. There will be a solution to this. They'll find it."

Belinda glanced around her as if suddenly nervous someone could be watching, but Bennett had no time to say anything about it before she moved on to the next topic. "Soon enough there'll be lemonade and hot dogs selling right over there."

Bennett followed her sight to the parking lot way at the other end of the beach. "I know it all too well."

"You frequent the lemonade and hot dog trucks too?"

"I certainly did in high school. Well, as a senior anyway."

"Temporary food obsession?"

"Temporary saving obsession." Bennett bent down and rinsed the shell in the water. "I worked in the lemonade truck, trying to save for college."

"Did it work?"

"Well, between that and waiting tables and other assorted jobs I took on when I could, I did make it work."

"If anyone could, it would be you." Belinda smiled, but it looked more melancholy. "It's so funny to think you were right over there all that time. You may have even sold me lemonade." She shaded her eyes, wrinkling her nose. "Did you have bleach blonde hair and wear the same red plaid shirt all that summer?"

Bennett shook his head just happy she still wanted to word play.

"Ah, well. I still bet we saw each other."

"You come to this beach?"

Belinda shrugged. "Why not?"

"You don't have a...private beach you like better?"

"I see how it is." Belinda grinned. "You think I'm a beach snob. Well, I am. And I prefer this beach. My family always has." She was now twirling the hoodie ties around her fingers. "What about your family? Do they live in the area?"

"My dad lives in-state." He was in a perfectly good mood; no need to ruin it. "And my grandmother lives right here in Portside."

She nodded in understanding, but Bennett could see she wouldn't be satisfied with that enigmatic response forever. He started to think—no, dared to hope—this little thing he had going might last longer than he initially imagined.

"I hate to leave already," Belinda said, "but I have a dinner thing to go to and I have to get ready."

"A dinner thing?" She was just waiting for him to ask, he could see it on her face, but he wanted her to stay as long as possible so he willingly obliged her.

"It's a thing for patrons of the art museum. My parents are big donors and I promised them I would represent. So I need to clean up."

From his vantage point, there was nothing special she needed to do to look any cleaner. Before he lost his courage, Bennett asked, "Are you going alone?"

Belinda blushed. "Kyle would go with me any other time, but not tonight. So, yeah, I'm going solo."

Bennett breathed a little easier, relaxing his shoulders. That was good news. Very good news.

"Can we catch up later?" Belinda said. "Tomorrow maybe?"

Bennett's eyes glinted. "We will definitely catch up later."

Chapter 12

Bennett swung by his house to shower and change to meet Jonas, but he still got there early. He spun a french fry between his fingers while he waited, involuntarily thinking about the leaf he plucked from Belinda's hair when he met her on the Ocean Walk. That afternoon felt like a long time ago now that he was concerned with helping her solve the issues with her brother. It was an interesting situation no matter how you looked at it, but he would stay on it to keep near Belinda even if it wasn't interesting.

Jonas pulled out the chair next to him, the screeching waking Bennett up from his reverie. Jonas grinned, snapping the plastic menu in front of him. "Dreaming of Fawn Eyes, Bennett?"

Bennett snarled, dropping the soggy fry back on the plate. "I'm thinking about the sticky situation she's in." And the unspoken thoughts on her face earlier, he thought.

Jonas' grin disappeared. "Well, her brother is certainly trapped in an unpleasant one, that's for sure. On all fronts. How was she after Kyle...you know?"

"Frantic. Nervous. Scattered." Bennett recalled her expression when he told her about the rental car. "She got a little...verklempt."

"Verklempt? So she did go hysterical....that took longer than I imagined."

"I wouldn't define it as hysterical. She just lost it when I told her about Kyle and the rental car business. Then she ran up into her room for a while."

"And went hysterical. Belinda ran into her room so you wouldn't see, but trust me. She went nuts once the door closed. If there's one thing I learned growing up with four women, it's what happens when they have meltdowns."

Bennett had to accept that Jonas did have an advantage over him when it came to women, having three sisters. He leaned on the table then leaned back when bread crumbs stuck to his forearm. "What do you make of the rental car business anyway?"

Jonas scanned the menu. "Kyle denies that he rented that car and got pretty upset at the suggestion that he hurt his own sister. We're in the process of hunting down actual witnesses who made the rental agreement and not just a piece of paper, but it's difficult because it's a local place and the owners are being all skittish. I don't know what they're afraid of, but whatever people. I just want to solve this case."

"Okay. So I've gotten the official statement. Now what do you actually make of it?"

Jonas grinned. "I don't buy it. I could believe he killed Jeff, but trying to kill his twin sister in a brutal car accident? No. I don't see it." He set his menu down.

"If he killed Jeff, he might be afraid that Belinda will find out. People do terrible things when they're desperate." Of course, he didn't buy Kyle as that kind of guy either.

"That's true enough. But I'm not sold yet." Jonas stared at him over the menu, slanting his green eyes. "You're holding back on me. What's up?"

Bennett pursed his lips. Sometimes he thought Jonas knew him a little too well. He had too much trouble hiding how he really felt around Jonas. "It's just a feeling I get whenever the whole subject of Mark comes up with Belinda."

"You think something was going on with Kyle and Mark's girl there, uh, Lily Devore?"

Bennett wished that's what it was. "No...with Belinda and Mark."

Jonas' eyes widened. "I did not think of that." Jonas arched his back, leaning away from the table. "Are you sure this isn't just you trying to find a major flaw in Belinda?"

"No. And I don't even care that much, but..."

"But?"

Bennett sighed. "But I hate feeling jealous of a dead man." Every time Belinda said Mark's name, his stomach twisted up, and it had finally hit him that he wanted her to say his name with as much feeling. It was annoying to say the least.

"Fear not. I don't think she's planning on going through life alone because of it." Jonas' phone buzzed. He checked it, glowered, and put it back in his pocket. "Catch up session ended I guess." He stood, the chair screeching again.

"One more thing before you go." Bennett tapped the table. "The address in the notebook I found at Belinda's? It belongs to a lawyer."

"Does that help us?"

"Not sure yet."

Jonas humphed. "We'll get to that later I guess. Eat some of those fries for me, won't you?" Jonas saluted and whirled back out of the restaurant.

Bennett stared at the soggy fries, now also cold, and turned up his nose. He was pretty sure even Jonas would pass them up. He checked the time, paid for his food, and ran out.

~ * ~

"You look nice," Kyle said as Belinda rounded the final stair in her black dress with the frilly skirt. It was Kyle's first attempt at talking since she came home, and he would have to pick now when she was running late for the art museum thing.

She thanked him and then they stood staring at each other awkwardly. Belinda really wanted to race out, but she also felt bad just taking off.

"I'm sorry," he said a minute later, his eyes darting between hers and the floor, the kitchen, the door. "About earlier."

It wasn't quite enough, but it would have to do for now. So she gave him a quick hug and promised they would talk more when she got back, which wouldn't be too late if she could help it. She started to pull away, but Kyle restrained her, placing his hand on her head. Belinda was too shocked to move, and he didn't say a word. Just kissed her forehead before letting her go.

"Be careful, little sister."

Belinda half-smiled and drifted out with Kyle waving with worried eyes as she closed the door behind her. She barely had time to wonder what on earth that had been about before she entered the closed museum now filled with mingling patrons and museum employees and volunteers.

Belinda accepted a champagne flute from a passing server in the hallway just in time to see Lily Devore in the exhibit room at the end of it. Belinda muttered to herself and slipped into the smaller room to her side. She already knew the pieces in there, but she looked at each oil painting as if she'd never seen any of them. Especially the painting of the sailboat at full tilt.

She stared at it in a trance, trying to decide what Kyle's odd hug had meant, when a wrinkled hand wrapped around her shoulder. Belinda jumped, eliciting a chuckle from the older man behind her. "I thought I was too old and creaky to startle anyone anymore." He smiled and side-hugged her.

Russell Carmichael. Well, it was better than Lily Devore.

"I've heard through the grapevine that you come to us straight from your grandmother's," he said silkily. "How is she since I saw her last anyway?"

The grapevine could only be one person. Belinda's nana was right. That old biddy was out to get her.

"Still not interested."

Carmichael threw his head back and cackled. Belinda couldn't believe he hadn't given up the chase yet. According to her nana, Carmichael had been after her for decades, if you counted the time before she married too. He waited a year after Belinda's grandfather died in the nineties before starting all over again. If she believed her nana, and Belinda did, it was more about her money. But who knew? Maybe Carmichael did really like her that much.

He sort of forced her out of the side room and toward the main exhibit area—a large box with wood floors and a vaulted ceiling. Several conversations echoed, but Belinda hung around the rim, deciding it was safer as both Lily Devore and Jarrett were in the center of the room. Events and fundraisers were dangerous places when you were on the outs with anyone in their general circle. She admired the gallery of paintings from a modern artist and a friend of her family's. Her mother owned several originals.

She made her way around the room, standing back a few feet to absorb one painting in particular. A few of the pieces on display were new to her, including this one. She glimpsed a man off to her side doing the same as she. With another, more studied, glance, Belinda twirled around to face Bennett. He leaned back on one leg with a hand stuck in his jeans' pocket and a decidedly smug look on his chiseled face as if he knew she'd be there.

"You..." she stammered. "You didn't tell me you'd be here!"

"I didn't know *you* would be here," Bennett said. "You said you had a dinner thingy, remember?"

Belinda pursed her lips. "Don't play dumb with me, gray-eyed eagle. You knew this is what I meant."

Bennett's eyes glinted. "So I did. Are you sorry to see me?"

Why did his cheekiness have to be so darn attractive? "I don't know why, considering how insolent you are, but I am glad to see you." He'd drawn much closer, but it felt comfortable now. "Actually, I'm relieved. I wasn't really in the mood to come."

"I'm sure everyone would understand if you stayed home tonight."

"Not everyone." She glanced at the floor.

"Well, you look beautiful. And like you attend these events often."

Belinda blinked. Had Bennett just said she was beautiful? "You don't look like a stranger here either." She looked him over, casual chic balancing a red wine glass in one hand.

"I'm not your parents, for certain, but I have my interests too."

"Are you a fan?" She jutted her chin toward the wall of canvas. Bennett nodded, his head tilted back to look at the painting above them. "Well, the next time my parents have Simone for dinner, I'll invite you so you can tell her in person."

Bennett arched an eyebrow. "I should have guessed."

Belinda smiled sheepishly and was about to add that she only mentioned it because of his interest in the artist's work when the museum director pulled her away to ask about her parents, kindly ignoring the news about Kyle, though she was sure they all knew. She glanced back but Bennett stayed on the perimeter of the room, returning to examining the paintings. On top of not being in the mood to chitchat, she was also now in the same circle with Lily, who glowered every time she made the mistake of glancing at her. She caught Jarrett's eyes once, but he averted his.

Cliffhanger

Belinda snagged a plate with shrimp, too hungry to be picky. She gave up on the miniature fork almost immediately, trying to eat delicately with her fingers. Just when she thought she'd succeeded at capturing one of the shrimps, the bugger squirted out of her hands and dive-bombed Lily, bonking her on the chin and free falling down her plunge V-neck dress.

Lily screeched and danced around in a circle as the shrimp used her stomach as a slip-n-slide. The entire group stopped to watch, Lily's squeals the only echo in the room. Belinda stared with her mouth agape.

"Belinda Kittridge!" Lily shrieked. If the entire room wasn't watching before, they were now. In fact, Belinda was pretty sure she heard people in the hallway actually enter the room. "Mark was a fool! How he ever dumped me. *Me*. For...for you is absurd!"

"Oh, dear," Carmichael muttered from somewhere nearby.

Belinda felt her face go hot as everyone turned their attention to her. A queasy, unsettled feeling writhed in her stomach. It could have been the concussion still, but she doubted it.

Lily's walnut eyes, filled with rage, appraised Belinda. Belinda glanced around her, but there was no one in that room any less shocked than her.

"I should go," Belinda managed to squeak out.

"You're not going anywhere."

There was that panic again.

"I have business with you, Belinda Kittridge. And you're not leaving until it's done."

Bennett came into Belinda's peripheral, making her jump.

Now if there was one person in that room who could go head-to-head with Lily it was Bennett Tate with his gray eyes now the color of cold steel. "Believe me," he said sharply, "you're done." With his hand firmly on Belinda's waist, he started to lead her out.

"Look at you!" Lily said to their backs. "Mark belonged to one of the top families in Portside, and you're sashaying around with some glorified mall cop who thinks donating a hundred dollars a year makes him one of us!"

Belinda froze despite Bennett's trying to push her forward. She whipped around, closing the distance between her and Lily in a few short strides. She had no idea what she looked like, but it must've been bad because the crowd parted for her like royalty. And not the waving to the crowd kind of royalty, but the off with their heads kind of royalty.

"Let me make something perfectly clear," Belinda hissed, close enough to Lily's face to smell the champagne on her breath. "Nobody talks to my friends that way. Least of all some lawyer's daughter whom my family could buy and sell five times over!"

Nobody moved. Nobody breathed. Nobody so much as swallowed.

Except Russell Carmichael who murmured that the Kittridges always did give the best parties. Belinda decided to put in a good word for him to her nana.

She left with Lily's eyes exploding out of her head, catching sight of Jarrett gawking at her as she breezed back the way she came. Belinda's heels were the only sound in the entire museum as the two of them walked out, every pair of eyes fixated on them.

Let them talk about that.

Chapter 13

Belinda fumed, spitting out half-articulated curses as Bennett walked her across the street to her car. He watched her in fascination. One minute she looked about ready to pass out, the next she had the entire room kneeling in her presence. And all it took was Lily Devore insulting him.

"You didn't have to defend me," Bennett said while she muttered to herself and dumped her purse out on her hood to find her keys. "I couldn't care less what any of them think about me."

Belinda huffed, slamming her clutch down in frustration. Not so good for the paint job, but he didn't dare tell her so. "I care what they think! You're not giving them money so you can hobnob. Look at you. You spent the entire night in a corner staring at the wall."

"Actually, I was—"

"You know, her family did that very thing. They bought their way into this circle. She has no right..." Belinda growled and stamped her foot. "I was fully prepared to write Simone a check when I got home."

"For what?"

"For slamming one of her paintings over Lily's head. The only reason I didn't is because I doubted I could lift one by myself and Victoria's not here to help."

"That's probably a good thing."

Belinda stopped huffing and throwing things and just stared at him, a little smile tugging at his mouth. "I don't normally act like this."

Bennett dug his hands into his pockets. "Is it true about your family?"

Belinda got closer. "I hate pulling rank, but it's the truth. In all honesty, I think part of Lily's anger comes from knowing good and well that Mark and I, economically, were equals. Dating Mark was sort of a social stepping stone for her and if he left her for me..." She shrugged. "I guess it might have hurt her socially too. You know what they say. Keep your friends close, the people with more influence than you closer."

"Was she using him?"

Belinda's eyes flickered, but the flames were burning out. "Mark thought so. You saw what just happened. When you truly care about position the way Lily Devore does, you know who you have to work with and make happy."

"Then apparently she doesn't. Look how she treats you."

"It does hurt her, you know. Even if she thinks it doesn't. My parents have contributed a lot to the Portside community beyond just money. People don't just respect them; they like them."

"That applies to you too."

Belinda folded her arms. "That's only because of my parents."

"It's because of you. When you walked out of that room, nobody saw the Kittridge's daughter. They saw Belinda."

"I threw my family's money in their faces. I never do that. My parents never do that. And anyway, you were the one who really stood up to Lily." She waved a hand in his direction. "You didn't need a bank account to get everyone in that room listening to you."

Bennett smirked. "She was right though. Not about how I feel about supposedly being one of them. I don't give them money for that purpose. I can and I want to. But in the end, I'm well aware my presence doesn't count for much."

"That's not true."

"Yes, it is. And you basically just said so yourself."

Belinda's arms dropped to her sides and she focused on the pavement. "I'm sorry," she whispered.

"I don't care," he said firmly. "My mom cares. But I don't." There was the slightest hint of bitterness in his voice.

"Do you see her a lot?"

Bennett hesitated. "Not so much. No." He laughed. But it was crisp, not playful. "Lily Devore and my mom fight their whole lives to command the sort of respect that you just come by naturally. All you had to do was throw food at somebody and you morphed into an aristocrat."

"I morphed into my grandmother." Belinda shook her head, not realizing it before. "I was with her too long."

"The grandmother you mentioned to Carmichael?"

Belinda nodded proudly. "Just sitting there she has everyone acting on their best behavior. She's incredible."

"It runs in the family."

Belinda flushed. He was going to say something else, but she didn't give him the chance.

She kissed him.

Belinda wrapped her arms around his neck, her fingers digging into his hair, sending chills down his spine.

"Thank you for standing up to Lily," she said softly when it was over.

Bennett was just trying to get the world spinning around him under control.

"I liked Mark but I blew my chances before he started dating Lily. And then..." Belinda still gripped his hair. "I'm not making that mistake this time."

She looked fully prepared to kiss him again and now Bennett was anchored and ready to go when a car zoomed across the road in the wrong direction down the one-way street they stood on. Bennett dove toward the sidewalk, taking Belinda right along with him. They watched the car screech left and then right across the next street and out of sight.

Bennett helped Belinda to her feet, his heart racing.

"I don't suppose you caught the license plate?" she said shakily.

Feet scampered toward them, the figure of Russell Carmichael temporarily lit up under the streetlamp. "Are you kids all right?"

Bennett nodded weakly.

"Phew!" Carmichael said, huffing and puffing. "Your family does know how to make an exit."

Belinda smiled wryly. "I'll tell my grandmother you said so."

~ * ~

After making sure Belinda got home safely and struggling to wind down enough to fall asleep, Bennett ran out of his bedroom, following the sound of banging on his front door. He opened to a wild-eyed Belinda, her jacket askew and hair half up and half down. He tried to rub the blur from his eyes, but she was still out of focus.

"You're not wearing pants," Belinda said flatly.

Bennett looked down, then up, frantically looking for something to hide behind. He dashed back to his bedroom, yanking jeans out of a drawer and hopping around his bed, trying to pull them on without crashing to the floor in the process. He stuffed his head through a T-shirt as he ran back.

"Kyle is missing!" she said before he could flick on a light. "I thought he was sleeping, but it hit me as I fell asleep that his Jeep wasn't in the driveway when I got home."

Bennett rubbed his eyes again. "I...I'm not quite getting you. Maybe he just hasn't gotten home yet." Bennett checked the clock over the mantle nearby. "It's just one in the morning."

Belinda stared at him like he'd gone crazy. "Where would he be?"

"Out with friends?"

"He doesn't have any friends!" Belinda threw her arms up. "He works, he comes home, he works. That's it. He's gotten completely antisocial."

Bennett shrugged. "He could be at a bar. He has had a lot of stress lately."

Belinda shook her head vigorously. "You don't know him. He's not out with friends; he's not at a bar. Something bad has happened to him. I can feel it." She pounded her chest, her eyes desperate. "Do you have any siblings?"

Bennett shook his head no.

"Well, I don't know how to describe this, but a twin is a sibling grown exponentially. We shared a womb. I know he's in trouble."

Bennett sucked in a breath and grabbed his phone and keys, waving Belinda through the open door. He got behind the wheel and started moving like he knew where to go. Belinda waited for him to say where they were going, but finally couldn't wait any longer and just asked.

"I think Kyle has been following you."

Belinda looked at him sideways. "As in trailing me or something? How do you know?"

"I've done a lot of trailing; I just do."

"Since when?"

"My guess is since the car accident. I think he knows something that we don't."

A new wave of panic lit up her eyes. "Oh, Bennett! That's what he's been hiding! All this time..." She buried her face in her hands. "That's why he was so emotional tonight...last night...you know what I mean."

"Emotional?"

"Right before I left for the stupid dinner at the museum, he apologized and hugged me. But it was a weird hug. Like he was...afraid."

Bennett sped up.

They whirled into the museum parking lot and Belinda got out, following Bennett blindly. "Why are we here?" she whispered as they ran around the building to the backyard.

"Because I saw Kyle's Jeep parked nearby on my way in."

"Why didn't you tell me?"

"I had no reason to at the time. And it was only a guess."

"Now it's not a guess?"

"Now it's not a guess."

They checked the yard, pretty open except for a few small bushes and a couple of sculptures. Bennett grunted, looking around. He couldn't have just waltzed inside. He had to be outdoors somewhere. Belinda watched him expectantly, gripping his arm. They scaled the grounds, Bennett waving his flashlight all around, to no avail. Belinda's growing panic traveled down to her fingernails, now pinching his skin.

"Maybe he was waiting in his car," Bennett said, his mind circling through the possibilities. What he would have done in that situation. "Or close enough to watch the building without being spotted by anyone inside." He chewed on his lip, his eyes roving from the museum to the park across the road.

They ran to the park, starting the search systematically from the top, checking all the potential hiding spots. But there was nothing. Not even any clear evidence of someone being there earlier. Bennett switched direction with Belinda clinging to him and they slowed up when Bennett found his Jeep. A whimper escaped from Belinda when he aimed his flashlight inside and lit up nothing. Absolutely nothing. She placed her hands on the window, peering inside as if that would conjure up Kyle's image.

"We'll find him," Bennett said dialing Jonas, more panicky then he wanted to let on. Especially when he caught sight of Kyle's phone on the Jeep's console.

"I don't understand. He's a suspect. Isn't that what the killer wants?"

"He may simply be getting too close to the truth." Bennett counted the rings before Jonas picked up. He was there within ten minutes, his clothes as mismatched as the two of them.

Bennett explained the situation with Belinda interjecting every few sentences. Jonas urged them to go home and try to rest. Officially, neither Bennett nor Belinda could help. So Bennett said she could sleep at his house that night and go home in the morning. But Belinda fought him, unraveling as tears slid down her face.

"Someone might call. I...I have to be there." Sobs swallowed up the last words as she crumpled into Bennett's arms. He looked to Jonas pleadingly.

Jonas placed a hand on her head, leaning over to see her face, half-smothered by Bennett's chest. "We need you, Belinda. You know Kyle better than anyone on this planet and we need your help to find him. But you won't be able to help us unless you're thinking clearly, am I right?"

Belinda squeaked out a yes.

"All right, then," Jonas said soothingly. "You go home with Bennett where you'll be safe and can sleep for a while. Then tomorrow you'll be ready to go."

Belinda lifted her head, managing a stiff nod.

"That's my girl." Some sort of silent understanding passed between Jonas and Bennett and Bennett took her back to his house.

Belinda denied that she could sleep, but oddly enough, she was gone minutes after hitting the pillow. Bennett, however, stared at the ceiling from the couch in the living room, his pulse racing. He kept checking to make sure she was safe, still curled up in a ball in his bed.

He couldn't let her see, but in the dark he had nothing to hide, and he let all of his fear surge through his body. He reviewed every detail of Jeff's murder so far, including just theories. Kyle had put something together, but what was it? What did he have that they were missing? And more worrying, did Belinda know it too? Bennett got off the couch to check on her again.

Chapter 14

Belinda sat down at the two-seater table just off of the kitchen shortly after first light. She'd pulled her hair back into a neat ponytail and wore slim-fitting jeans and a zippered hoodie that brought out the pink in her cheeks. And why Bennett was taking such close notice of all of this, he couldn't fathom. Aside from looking a little piqued, she looked a ton better than he felt.

"Did you sleep well?" he said, already knowing she slept decently because he checked on her about every hour.

Belinda nodded, giving him a strangled affirmative. "Did you?"

Bennett hesitated. He didn't want to let on that he'd been watching her sleep. "Uh...not really."

Her brown eyes grew sad. "I would've taken the couch."

Now he'd made her feel bad. Great. He blew it off and changed topics. "Would you like anything?" His empty fridge flashed through his mind. "Orange juice? Water? Coffee?" *Please don't ask for food*, he thought desperately.

She brightened at his last offering. "Coffee sounds wonderful."

Bennett nodded, pleased he could at least deliver coffee, which seemed to make her happy at all times. He measured grounds into a filter, counting them off in his head, trying to think of something to say or ask.

"You have a lovely house," Belinda said quietly, beating him to it. But she was better at that than he was. "I tried to imagine what sort of house a Bennett Tate would live in, and I have to say you have much better taste than I gave you credit for."

Bennett pressed the power button on the coffee maker, enraptured by what she was saying. She had imagined what his house looked like. "It's not an Ocean Ave. house, but I like it well enough."

Belinda's cheeks glowed pinker like she was embarrassed. "I...I knew your house would be nice," she yanked on the hem of her sleeves, "but I was just surprised by the architecture."

Somehow he'd already managed to say something wrong, but he wasn't positive what it was. "What did you expect exactly?"

Again, he said something wrong because she continued to look embarrassed. "Oh, I'm not sure I had a specific house style in mind. I like the whole shingled bungalow look. It's...it's artistic."

Bennett raised one of his thick eyebrows, determined to say something right while he pulled out a cereal box he'd forgotten about. "Now who knows her architecture?"

Belinda half-smiled, the rose color in her cheeks diminishing to a modest baby pink. "Are you remodeling? It looks like you're doing some work to the outside."

He placed sugar and cream in front of her and then realized he probably should ask what she takes in her coffee. "I bought it as sort of a fixer-upper. It doesn't need major work, just some TLC."

"And you're the one to provide it?"

"Me and my paintbrush."

Belinda leaned on the tabletop, her eyes rather hollow. "It's nice and quiet over here. Is it like this all summer or does it turn into Grand Central Station once tourism picks up?"

"We'll find out for sure pretty soon. I explored this area thoroughly last summer and it seemed relatively quiet even at the height of tourism."

Belinda dumped gracious amounts of sugar into her mug and stirred. "So is this your first summer in Portside?"

Bennett was still reviewing the fact that she liked his house. "No, but it will be my first summer in this house. I've lived in Portside for a few years. I used to room with Jonas actually." Belinda nodded and sipped her coffee. Apparently, it was his turn. "Does your neighborhood turn into Grand Central Station in summer?"

"Surprisingly, no. And we're right near the beach too. However, the street Victoria lives on has a constant flow of traffic the entire summer. Her husband hates it."

Bennett frowned. "I don't think I'd like that."

Belinda's eyes twinkled and she cocked her head to the side thoughtfully. "You know, I've wondered how many parties and events I've been to that you've—secured—before we met."

"Haven't you been gone for a while?"

"Yeah, but I visit sometimes, mostly to see Victoria, and we go to things. So we could have crossed paths a few times now and never known it."

Bennett set his eyes firmly on hers. "Is that a good thing or a bad thing?"

Her twinkle increased. "A good thing, definitely."

Satisfied that Belinda meant it, Bennett turned his attention to the envelope she'd set on the table. Belinda took that as her cue to explain. "I found these photos, and many more just like them, in Lily's dresser at her family's house." Belinda exhaled.

Bennett raised his eyebrows, studying the two photos of Belinda and...

"Mark," Belinda answered, reading his mind. "That's Mark. It's probably nothing." She pushed a loose string of hair behind her ear, keeping her eyes on the envelope.

Bennett held up the two photos, looking at Mark a little closer. He frowned. Mark was better looking than he'd imagined. "You say there were more like these?"

"A lot more."

"Then this is not nothing, Belinda. This is surveillance."

"Are you sure?"

Bennett glanced at the photos. The telephoto lens. The hiding-in-a-bush feel. The uninhibited acting of the subjects. "Oh, yeah. I'm sure."

Belinda hid her face in her hands, using every ounce of energy to suppress the meltdown that wanted to explode out of her. After a few minutes, she wiped away a few stray tears and faced him squarely. "What do we do?"

"We go back to your house, and we trust Jonas."

"Is that all we can do? I mean..." Belinda rubbed her eyes.

Bennett put up a hand to signal for her to wait as his phone buzzed. After a couple of minutes of listening to Mr. Trebor talk in incomprehensible circles, Bennett finally calmed the older man down enough to find out why he was so worked up. The bottom line was that Trebor needed to talk to him as soon as possible. After promising several times over that he would meet him at the shop later that morning, Bennett returned to the table, consumed by what he'd gleaned from his conversation with Trebor.

"What's the matter?" Belinda said.

"I'm not a hundred percent sure. Mr. Trebor is excitable." Bennett smirked, thinking about the woman across from him. "But he sounded serious. Could be about the accident."

Belinda almost choked on her powdered donut.

"Don't get excited," Bennett said. "I don't know if that's true. I got surveillance and Kittridge from his babbling."

Belinda sipped some coffee to swallow the donut successfully. Bennett found the donuts next to the cereal, but they were stale. "There are two other things I should tell you," she said.

Bennett's eyes shot up from his coffee stirring.

"I found a lump of cash in Jarrett's backpack when he visited me at Victoria's, and I think someone uninvited was in my house." She said the last part quickly, keeping her eyes on anything but Bennett.

Bennett slammed his coffee mug on the table. "What?"

Belinda winced. "I found a suspicious mud print by the side door after you left. It wasn't there when you arrived and no one I know of would have left it."

Bennett ran his hands over his head. "I really wish you had mentioned this earlier."

"I didn't touch it. It should still be there on the floor." Belinda licked powdered sugar from her lips. "So...you go talk to Mr. Trebor and I'll, you know, go do my thing."

"If by your thing you mean staying at home until I get back, then yes."

Belinda batted her eyelashes. "Of course that's what I mean."

Bennett watched her closely. He didn't believe for a moment that's what she intended to do, but he would take measures to ensure it's what she actually did. The stakes were higher now. He thought briefly about her kiss from the night before. Now was no time to get into it, but the quicker they figured all of this out, the faster they could get on to other matters.

Bennett took her home and waited like a guard while she showered, examining the muddy footprint. It was a sneaker. Probably a canvas sneaker. He contemplated that as Belinda came down the stairs, apparently expecting him to just leave her there. Instead, he offered to help carry something into the carriage house. He knew she still had more work to do.

They didn't have room for all the boxes plus their bodies in the carriage house without creating a fire hazard, so she led him to the small garden shed on the opposite side of the property. Bennett set his boxes where she pointed and walked out in front of her. Before Belinda could get out of the shed, Bennett snatched the handle and forced the door shut, locking it from the outside.

"Bennett!" Belinda screeched. "What are you doing?"

"I'm trying to keep you from any more danger. I'll call Jonas to come get you out after I go, all right?"

"No, I'm not all right!" Belinda huffed. "You've just locked me in the garden shed!"

"It's for your own good." Bennett peeked at her through the side window. Boy was she steamed. He chuckled, making her eyes flash that much more. "You won't be here long, I promise."

"You bet I won't."

Bennett half-smiled. "Be good. I'll see you soon."

"Be—"

Bennett left her stewing, dialing Jonas on his way out. "Yeah, I have a favor to ask though you could be in physical danger doing it." Bennett's mouth crooked up. "You need to release a certain someone from her garden shed. And then, you need to scope out her house for a possible break in." He could still hear Belinda fussing on the other side of the driveway and hurried off to town.

Bennett took the back side entrance into Trebor's shop because of the yellow tape still blocking the front door due to the accident. Other then some makeshift plywood, nothing had changed. It was quiet inside and Bennett hoped Trebor hadn't forgotten about their meeting. He'd locked Belinda in a garden shed for this.

He walked into the back office, hoping to find him just taking a nap or something. But Bennett stopped cold in the entrance to the office. Mr. Trebor's head was flat on top of his keyboard, blood streaming down through the keys and onto the desk. Bennett's stomach flip-flopped and he fumbled to get his phone from his pocket. As he struggled to articulate what had happened to the operator, Bennett realized the monitor above Trebor was zoomed in and frozen on a piece of security footage.

He stood as close as he dared for evidence's sake and for the sake of not being able to stand to see Mr. Trebor like that. But Bennett was right. It was a scene from Belinda's car accident. And there was a blood smear over part of the screen. He couldn't be certain, but from where he stood, Bennett felt positive someone was hiding behind the streak—watching the accident.

~ * ~

Belinda muttered a string of curses and insults to the air. Bennett was already long gone, but it made her feel better. No doubt he was grinning all the way to wherever he was headed, knowing that she was trapped in the shed wanting to choke him, which only made her more infuriated.

She plopped into the plastic seat and watched the dust particles floating by in the ribbons of sunlight coming in through the window. Belinda hadn't really processed what happened the night before, unless you counted the humiliating breakdown she'd had on Bennett's chest. Somehow, she'd slept dreamlessly the night before and didn't think about the whole situation until her eyes popped open and it all came crashing down on her. Her stomach twisted into knots and she felt too jittery to just lie there.

It was time to get serious.

There was no way she could just sit there waiting—for what?—while her brother was missing. So Belinda picked up a hoe and hacked through the side window. Then she climbed on top of the wooden table and used gardening gloves to clear away all the leftover glass. With a deep grunt she pushed up and through the window, just squeezing through with a lot of sucking in and pushing and flailing.

Once she was up and dusted off, Belinda ran upstairs to her bedroom to change. As she rearranged her hair, the lights went out. "You have got to be kidding me." Belinda tried several lights in different spots of the house and let out a long, irritated groan. At best, something tripped.

Belinda turned on a flashlight, aiming down the basement stairs. Maybe she should have stayed in the garden shed after all. Then she wouldn't feel obligated to deal with the power situation. Belinda took one step at a time, not in a hurry to enter the dark pit of their unfinished basement. It was just a holding tank for unwanted junk. And the circuit board, unfortunately. She tried not to think too hard about what could be crawling around her and scurried to the circuit panel, flinging the metal door open. At a glance, nothing was tripped. As she carefully inspected each breaker, the door to the basement slammed shut.

Belinda whirled around, her heart stopping for a beat. She aimed her light at the door and then jerked it around the rest of the room, holding her breath. Deciding it wasn't worth it, she darted for the stairs just as the circuit panel buzzed, sparked, and caught fire. Belinda screamed, glancing around the room in panic for anything that could help. She grabbed a blue tarp and started hitting it against the circuit board, but it wasn't stopping the blaze. There was nowhere for the fire to spread really, but the smoke started to burn her lungs.

She dropped the tarp and ran around the basement searching for anything else that could help. An old lamp? Nope. Her parents' bikes? Nope. Her dad's power tools? Nope. Belinda's heart raced as she ran around, the smoke spreading out from the circuit board. It stung her eyes even from a distance.

Belinda ran up the stairs, slamming into the door when it didn't open. She jangled the knob, but it was definitely locked. Panic took over and she twisted the knob pointlessly. The car accident, Kyle missing...someone was trying to kill her.

She ran back down, running around again to find something that she could use to put out the fire. Then she looked up. A window. One small, almost pointless window. Maybe she could do what she did in the garden shed, but she needed a boost.

She picked up a mop and slid a lawn chair across the concrete floor and stood on top, closing her eyes as she jabbed the mop handle into the glass. It took more force than she thought it would, but she finally broke through. Unlike the shed, she knew she wouldn't be able to squeeze her butt through this window, but she could breathe clean air and scream for help.

She poked her face out, inhaling the fresh air and then yelled with all her strength. But after screaming her lungs out, she started to despair. Who would be around to hear her? Most of their neighbors were still away, and even if their landscapers were working with the spread of land between houses...

She banged on the basement door again, yelling for help, and pushing and jangling the knob as smoke reached her. Pulling her shirt up over her mouth, she body slammed the door with her shoulder, yelling in pain, but trying again. Her eyes stung and she could taste the smoke on her tongue. Belinda could see the fire starting to lick out to other objects in the room. She coughed, still hoping to make the solid door give. This was absolutely the worst trip home. Ever.

After she tried forcing the door free for the umpteenth time, she jogged back down to find some sort of tool to force the door open. Before that, Belinda breathed deep through the window, trying to yell, but losing her voice quickly. She found a hammer and took the prying end of it to try to make the door give. As she pulled, flattening her foot against the wall for leverage, the door gave and Belinda toppled into the main house face first, hacking up a lung and blind, so relieved that the door had finally let go.

But then arms lifted her up and carried her outside where sirens deafened her and someone slipped a mask on her face and breathing grew easier and her lungs felt less irritated and her eyes cleared. Then she could see the features of Jonas Parker looming down on her, frowning but relieved.

"That was you?" she croaked. Jonas nodded. "I thought I was awesome and forced the door open."

"You get an A for trying," he said soberly. "You have bruises to prove it."

Belinda groaned. "You have to solve this case before I'm deformed."

"And you have to start listening when you're told to stay put."

Touché. "How did you get in?"

He smiled apologetically. "I'm afraid I had to bust through the glass on the back door."

"Add it to the list of renovations." At this point, some broken glass was the least of her worries. Beyond the chaos, Belinda could just make out a figure moving toward them in a hurry from the street.

Bennett breathed heavy, his face shiny with perspiration, but when he took her hand it was cold. "Thank you, Jonas. Thank you." He squeezed her hand.

Jonas quietly examined the edge of her stretcher.

"Do I have to go to the hospital again?" Belinda said through the mask, which garbled her question.

Jonas nodded. "It's a good idea after inhaling smoke."

Belinda's eyes watered up. Kyle wasn't around to sit with her.

"I'll come with you," Bennett said eagerly, "and I'll call Victoria."

Belinda choked on a sob she couldn't quite stifle. Bennett sandwiched her hand between both of his while Jonas placed a hand on her head.

"Is there anything we can do for you, sugar?" Jonas said.

"My parents," Belinda managed to get out. "They don't know...and I want them to know." A fresh set of tears washed down her face. Jonas patted her head, promising they would get a hold of them.

Bennett pecked her on the forehead and stepped away with Jonas reluctantly, keeping Belinda in sight.

"Do you know what was on that image on the screen?" Jonas' voice turned more urgent and concerned now that Belinda was out of earshot. His green eyes constricted with worry.

"It could be a person watching the accident," Bennett said quietly. "But I couldn't tell who."

"I'm wondering what set him off to look at the footage, and I'm told he delivers bouquets to his wealthier customers. I'm wondering if Trebor was motivated to go back to the footage because of something he found out by making house calls."

Bennett glanced at Belinda, looking like a lost puppy on the stretcher in the middle of her yard. "What about the other shop cameras?"

"On it right after this. And just to warn you, I couldn't care less about procedure right now. Whatever I find, I want your eyes all over it."

Chapter 15

Bennett took Belinda to the Ocean Walk the next afternoon. He reasoned that she could use some fresh salt air after inhaling smoke from a fire, but he acted suspiciously and Belinda figured something more was at work than her oxygen supply. She forced a smile and tugged playfully at the edge of his newsboy cap. Then her lips curled down.

"I forgot," she said, crossing her arms. "I'm still mad at you."

"I'll take it, considering you're still alive."

Belinda's joy evaporated thinking about that. "Poor Mr. Trebor. Do you know what happened?"

Bennett summarized what he'd seen, skipping how he died. As he spoke, his whole countenance turned down. "I know Jonas won't overlook anything, but I just...I feel responsible."

Belinda wanted to blow away the cloud that screened his expression. "Why? You have nothing to do with this."

"I drew attention to the footage on his cameras."

"The police would have checked that out anyway."

"I know, but...maybe I got him thinking."

"Whoever killed him wouldn't have known about all that."

"Necessarily."

Belinda frowned, skipping down a set of stairs to the path, squishing to the right to let some oncoming foot traffic pass. Bennett strolled behind her, trying to keep his eyes on the back of her head and not on other pieces of her anatomy that popped out at him with every step.

"Guess where my favorite place is," Belinda said, hoping to distract him.

Cliffhanger

"The gelato place in town?"

Belinda wrinkled her nose. "You're just being cheeky."

Bennett lifted his brows, his eyes flicking down her back. "It's coming up. Don't fall asleep back there."

The Walk spread out and opened up into a half-moon lookout. The cliffs jutted out, offering a clear view of the Atlantic. Belinda jogged to the lookout, leaning her palms on the stone wall guarding it and waved for Bennett to hurry up. "Look at that," she said. "Now that is the crown jewel of Portside."

Bennett caught up to her, shading his eyes to see what the jogging was for. The emerald green water rippled out toward the horizon.

"Doesn't the water just look like it stretches out forever without any land blocking its path?" Belinda stood on her toes, though she didn't need to. "When I stand here, I understand why people took to the sea to explore it. Even knowing good and well what's out there, I still want to jump on a boat and see for myself." Her eyes grew romantic and misty.

Bennett admired the view, but he admired Belinda admiring the view more. She grabbed his forearm, dragging him to another entrance and down a set of stairs to the bottom of the cliff where the waves steamrolled over the rocks, frothing at the edges. What had been a din became a roar at the bottom of the stairs. Belinda clasped her hands behind her back, looking out at the endless water, more melancholy than she'd been minutes earlier. "The police just think Kyle ran, don't they? That he's guilty and he took his opportunity and ran." Her face tightened as she struggled to keep the tears in.

With the chaos and her fear, Bennett felt bad telling her, but she had a right to know. "He took out a large sum of money the other day, and leaving his phone and car behind would just make good sense."

"But why leave it near the museum?"

Bennett kept his gaze on the water below. "Maybe he just wanted to make sure you were safe first."

Belinda closed her eyes. Kyle wouldn't just leave her. Would he? She purged that doubt immediately. Kyle would never run like that without telling her. They had very few secrets, and while she knew he had kept something from her lately, it wasn't that. If no one else wanted to look at other angles, then she would. Belinda raised her hand.

The corner of Bennett's mouth sloped up. "Yes?"

"What about the guy in the hallway?"

"The guy in the hallway?"

"Victoria and I passed one of your guys upstairs near the balcony where we saw Jeff in the gazebo."

Bennett tilted his head, squinting in thought. "I didn't have a guy upstairs near the balcony, though it could have been Finnegan." Bennett described his colleague in the most detail he could manage. Before he'd even finished, Belinda was shaking her head with her eyes closed.

"Nope," she said. "The guy that we saw was tallish and stocky with a shaved head and kind of a big nose."

Recognition flashed in his eyes. "Nobody like that works for me."

"Are you sure?" He'd recognized the description she gave him. Belinda had no doubt.

Bennett shifted his eyes sideways.

"Sorry. Gray-eyed eagle. Blah blah blah."

"I know who works for me and nobody with that description works for me."

"Then who was it?"

"It could have just been another guest."

Belinda shook one of her feet out of the flats she'd worn. They were cute, but she was starting to hate them. "Like I said, he looked like he was in some sort of official capacity. What if he was pretending to be one of your guys?"

"Then we would have a bigger problem."

"Tell me about it. There's some bald guy out there pretending to work for you."

"I was thinking more along the lines that we have an extra guest at the party that night who's unaccounted for." Bennett looked her right in the eyes, his own somber. "I have something I need to ask you."

Belinda's face fell. "That doesn't sound too pleasant."

"This whole business with Lily Devore. It's got something to do with your history." Bennett met her eyes straight on again. "Were you...involved...with Mark Nichols?"

Belinda felt her whole face and neck go up in flames. Even in the wind. She closed her eyes and took in a long breath. This was not the conversation she'd planned to have with Bennett that afternoon. "Mark spent a lot of time with us the summer after senior year, right before he died." Bennett nodded. "Okay, well, that wasn't exactly new. He and Kyle had been best friends for a long time, so I'd spent my fair share of time with him."

Belinda took a moment to compose what came next. It was so embarrassing having to tell this story to Bennett. "I think Mark was surprised that I was all for their sailing adventures, and he told me that Lily had threatened to break up with him if he chose the sailing."

"How did he react?"

Belinda's face turned an even deeper shade of red. "He...he told her to go ahead."

Bennett looked at her questioningly after several seconds of silence. "Because....because he wanted to be with you."

Belinda took another deep breath, unprepared to answer that question.

"Is that the entire story?" Bennett said, doubt lacing his words.

"Only Lily knows what really happened between them, and I'm not sure I can trust her version. She never caused any public scenes because she didn't want anyone to know, though I suspect Stellan knew what was going on. She still made it perfectly clear to me that she thought I was a boyfriend-stealing trollop. That's sort of where the trouble with Jeff began."

"How so?"

At least the worst of her story was over, and Bennett didn't seem phased. "He defended me. To Lily's face, which takes some, you know, guts."

Bennett smirked.

"Anyway, whenever I saw Jeff that summer, he acted kind of distant. I knew he liked me and I'd tried to dance around it all through high school."

"He liked you all through high school and never made a move?"

Belinda shrugged. "Jeff was a slow boil kind of person."

"Apparently," Bennett muttered.

"But that summer, he acted differently and looking back I think he suspected Mark and I liked each other."

"Did you?"

Belinda flushed all over again. "I...I liked him."

Bennett looked away.

"So...so Jeff was kind of my savior after the fact, and I think my reaction unintentionally encouraged him." Belinda sighed heavily. "He was already so unstable at that point because of Mark and then he finally just came out and told me he liked me."

"He snapped?"

Belinda nodded. "It was awful. Kyle just sort of vented all of his anger on Jeff, but I felt sorry for him. I didn't want to hurt him like that." Belinda's eyes filled with tears. "Not after everything he'd been through."

"He needed help, Belinda. Not a girlfriend."

She nodded, whispering, "I know."

Bennett shifted his weight. "Why...why did you kiss me that night? Did you actually want to or was it just rebellion because of what Lily said?"

Belinda turned her body to face him, putting her sunglasses on her head. She had two red imprints where the glasses met her nose, and a sprinkling of freckles that surfaced since they got there. But Belinda was still the loveliest thing he'd laid eyes on. "Why would you even ask that?"

Bennett looked away. "I...I misjudged someone's motives once. I'm more careful now."

"Was she rich?"

Bennett looked surprised, even through his glasses.

"It's just little things sometimes," Belinda said, "made me wonder. I worried that I was coming across as a snob and making you feel bad."

"No, never." Bennett licked his lips, his mouth feeling dry. "I just wanted to see how you'd react sometimes. There were signs before, you see, but I missed them."

"Have I passed your test so far?" Her heartbeat was close to drowning out the sound of the waves.

"With flying colors. I was almost a hundred percent sure but—"

"I went and kissed you and ruined everything." Belinda turned back toward the water. She was unsure if she was more irritated with him or herself for being so impulsive. "With Mark I was too late. With you..." She shrugged.

"Jonas keeps telling me I'm too paranoid."

"Well, you are."

"I'm sorry."

"You should be." All this time she'd really believed they were on the same page, and she'd opened her heart to him at every turn, clueless that he felt her money made her untrustworthy. "That's the only time I've gone and kissed some guy before he's so much as asked me out, and this is what I get. Generalized."

"You haven't spoken too highly of your own kind either."

Belinda balked. "My own kind? What are we? Baboons?"

"Some of you."

Her eyes flashed. "That's completely different."

"How?"

"I know them. I can say whatever I like."

"So as long as you know people, it's okay to generalize them?"

Belinda put her hands on her hips, her skin prickling at his baseless judgments. "From where I stand, *you're* the one acting like the baboon. I didn't judge you based on other men—especially the jerks—in the same economic bracket. And I took you to be more open minded than that."

He'd removed his sunglasses and now Bennett's eyes flashed. She'd insulted him. Good.

They both gazed out into the water in silence for a long time, Belinda trying to focus on other things. After a while, she tapped Bennett's shoulder, pulling him out of some deep thoughts no doubt, and pointed at a cavern in the rock face. "Pirate treasure hideaway?" she said, hoping to lighten the mood.

"Would be pretty hard to reach with the tide," he said flatly, not even looking that way. "Not to mention it might get washed away."

Belinda sighed. "You think too much."

"I will take that as a compliment."

"And I will remember to ask you for advice before I hide my stolen treasure."

Bennett returned her to Victoria's, neither of them saying anything on the ride there. As she got out, Bennett seemed like he wanted to say something, but he only said good-bye and that they'd meet up with Jonas somewhere later. Disappointed, Belinda returned to the safe haven of Victoria's with the rest of her own kind.

Cliffhanger

~ * ~

It seemed like such nonsense at that point, but Belinda needed to tackle packing up for the move to the carriage house, so Victoria went with her to help out. Belinda stared into Kyle's room, screwing up her mouth in disgust at the clothes and plates and glasses and who-knows-what strewn over the floor and tabletops. For some unknown reason, he'd made his bed. But that was her brother.

"Come on," Victoria said, putting her arm around Belinda. "Let's get this over with."

Belinda tiptoed into the sunlit dining room, the door Jonas busted through boarded up, and stared at the hutch. Or, more to the point, at the stemware and fine china behind the glass doors. Why did people always own all of this? Other than for ultra special occasions, it was too delicate and too fussy to bother with. She made a pouty face to get her desire to whine out of her system and she and Victoria got down to business.

"I want all the details," Victoria said, readying some newspaper. "And I think we should start with the plates."

Belinda gently released an almond colored plate from the wood rack, handing it to Victoria to tuck in a sheet of paper. Her mother hated those plates, each with a giant mauve flower in the center, but she had been stuck with them since she got married when her own mother demanded she pick out a set. Belinda had always wondered why her mother didn't just ditch them for new ones later, but she seemed to have a strange sentimental attachment to them that Belinda couldn't figure out.

"Well, I think I already told you everything I know at this point."

"Not those details, silly! I want Bentails!"

"Bentails?" Belinda laughed. She gave Victoria the scant updates she had and the highlight of the moment was definitely the newsboy cap. She left out the part where she kissed him. She didn't know if it would go anywhere after that last conversation.

"Belinda, how very personal of you, tugging on his cap." Victoria didn't know the half of it. It felt like nothing to Belinda after lip locking with him in the middle of the street.

"It happened involuntarily. I did not mean to do that."

"It didn't seem to bother him."

No, that didn't seem to bother him, but neither did the kiss until they started talking about it. Belinda rotated one of the crystal bar glasses, creating a rainbow on the wall. They were close to the only things in that cabinet that regularly saw the outside world. "I told him about Mark."

"Doesn't he already know about the accident?"

Belinda raised her eyebrows.

"Oh...you mean...oh..." Victoria nodded. "And?"

"He was very chill about the whole thing."

"Excellent."

"Then he told me he's prejudiced against rich women." Belinda gave her the gist of the conversation, surprising herself with how detached she sounded. "I guess he wouldn't care too much for the story behind these being that it involved our kind and all." Belinda carefully encased one of the bar glasses in tissue paper, and gently set it down in a box especially for them.

"He got burned obviously. He'll come around."

Belinda shrugged and reached for another bar glass, but it slipped from her grasp, spinning toward the wood floor in slow motion. Belinda recoiled as it shattered at her feet, the sound splitting through her skull. Neither of them moved, and Belinda stared helplessly at the shards of crystal scattered around them.

"I'll go get the vacuum," Victoria said.

"What am I supposed to tell them?"

Victoria stopped mid-step. "It's just a glass, Bels."

"It's not just a glass!" Belinda's voice escalated to a shriek and she picked up one of the shards, shaped like an icicle, and held it up. "It's a special honeymoon glass. The ones my dad searched Europe for and spent oodles of money to buy because nobody sold them in Paris and he wanted Mom to have a complete set!" Belinda started to choke. "How am I supposed to tell them that I broke one?"

Victoria pulled her up from the floor, forcing Belinda into a seat. "What's going on here with Kyle is not your fault."

"It's all my fault." Belinda covered her face. "I should never have..." She sobbed, Victoria stroking her hair and whispering it would be okay. "We're a matching set. How am I supposed to—"

"Shh." Victoria held her tight, trying to get her to think more positively. "You haven't lost Kyle. It's not going down like that. It's just not. You're supposed to meet up with Bennett and the detective later, right?"

Belinda nodded, catching tears dripping off her chin. "We couldn't come up with a meeting place though."

"They could come to my house."

Belinda blinked. "Are you serious?"

"Sure! Come on over after dinner. I'll have Dan pick up something for dessert." Victoria smiled, dabbing at Belinda's eye with a tissue.

"You just want to see him in his newsboy cap."

"You know it."

Belinda smiled. "He did look awfully cute."

"Mmm...happy thoughts." Victoria kissed her forehead.

The doorbell rang and they both jumped. Belinda rolled her eyes and got up to answer while Victoria dug out the vacuum.

It was Stellan of all people, and he didn't look too good. Haggard and sallow like he hadn't slept in days, but he seemed sincerely concerned about Belinda and her brother. He chewed on his lip after Belinda let it slip that the police suspected Kyle fled to Rio. Or, wherever. Rio just sounded good. She didn't really mean to say that, but she was tired and it was too hard to control herself.

"I spent a lot of time with Kyle on a small space," Stellan said moments later, "and I can't see him running. We disagreed a lot, and if there's one thing I learned about him, it's that he's not afraid to go head-to-head."

Belinda felt like there was more that he wanted to say.

"Can I help you move anything?" Stellan glanced at the boxes nearby.

Surprised, Belinda mumbled something and Stellan stacked a couple of boxes in his arms and trailed after her through the front yard and into the carriage house, which had the same gambrel-style roof as the main house and had a loft bedroom and open downstairs, including a kitchen and bathroom.

"Why was Jeff here anyway?" Belinda said. They set the boxes all the way in the back and returned for more. "He didn't tell me."

Stellan looked surprised at that remark. Maybe he didn't know that she'd spoken to Jeff again. "Jeff knew I'd be in town for the reunion, and he wanted to see me."

"He couldn't visit you in New York?"

"I think it was just good timing for him. Portside or New York—it's pretty much the same difference coming from San Francisco."

Belinda cocked her head to the side. "So he didn't come for some other reason?"

"Such as?"

"I'm not sure, but he was worried about something."

Cliffhanger

Stellan kept quiet behind her, picking up another box. "Business, probably. I know the work stress got to him."

Belinda tilted her head. "No, I'm pretty sure it was more on a personal level."

"How can you be sure?"

"Because he asked to talk to me. We had an appointment for the next day."

Stellan's box slipped from his grip and he tried to get a firmer hold on it by tapping it back into place with his knee. "Did he say what he wanted to talk about?" Stellan sounded pretty nervous, and Belinda couldn't say she didn't enjoy that to a degree.

"No specifics, but he really didn't want anyone to overhear. Or even see him talking to me I think."

Stellan lost his balance and after bouncing around a few times, both boxes crashed on the ground right in front of the carriage house. Belinda set her boxes down and dashed over, muttering under her breath. Stellan apologized, trying to help salvage the items that toppled out. His forehead looked damp, and his hands were shaking.

"Are you all right?" Belinda shoved the items back into the box. At least it was just all of Kyle's swill.

Stellan's mouth gaped in a smile. "I think I'm turning into Jeff."

"Why would that happen?"

Stellan laughed nervously, playing with the edges of a notebook on top of the pile.

"Stell," Belinda hesitated. It might be a risky move, but with Kyle missing... "I overheard you and Jeff talking at the party. You told him to stick with the original plan and keep quiet."

Stellan swallowed. "So you know."

Belinda's eyes widened, but she tried to stay cool.

Stellan closed his eyes. "I'm glad actually. I should have let him talk a long time ago."

"Maybe...maybe it's time for that."

Stellan nodded, picking up a random piece of rope in Kyle's belongings. "Mark was already dead when Jeff and I got there."

Chapter 16

The news that Stellan and Jeff got to *Sea Stud* early that morning to find Mark already dead in the water nearly made Belinda pass out. But it got better. Scared out of their wits, Stellan, against Jeff's better judgment, decided that they should go out as planned and then call for help out on the water and pretend like it was an accident.

Belinda's skin turned gray as Stellan told his story. "Why didn't you just call the police?" Belinda said, wanting to pull Stellan's hair out. And her own. She had been so stupid.

"I was scared. Mark and I had a pretty open blowout at the club earlier that week. I didn't think they'd believe us. Besides, it could have been an accident."

Belinda had forgotten about their fight. "Did you fight about Mark's plans with Kyle?"

"What? No." Stellan looked confused. "It was business-related. I wanted him to invest in something, but he refused and got kind of angry about the whole thing."

"Maybe because it was illegal?"

Stellan looked shocked.

"Honestly, Stell. Did you think we all thought you were squeaky clean? I'm taking it you managed to get Jeff involved in something more recently."

"I think he wanted out." He averted his eyes, but he looked sad.

"I should hope so. And you should get out too, before someone kills you."

Stellan drew his lips out into a hard line. "I don't think that's why he died."

"Was it because of Mark? Maybe Jeff knew who killed him. Have you thought of that? Maybe that's why he was such a wreck. And none of us...none of us would give him the time of day."

Belinda wanted to pick up one of the boxes and throw it across the yard. And then she did. Stellan just watched as she heaved Kyle's box of junk and tossed it into the air. She probably intended to hurl it like a football to the other side of the green near the garden shed, but it wound up just a few feet away, froze on its side for a few seconds and then plummeted right side up, most of the stuff still inside. It was more noise than mess.

Victoria came running out of the front door to see what had happened. Belinda kicked at the objects on the ground, but her aim failed and most barely moved from their original positions.

"I think she's having some sort of meltdown," Stellan said.

Victoria glared at him. "Of course she is idiot." Victoria stood back as Belinda flung her leg out. "What happened, sweetie? You had calmed down a few minutes ago."

"It's me," Stellan said quickly. "I've upset her." He retrieved something from his back pocket with his other hand and gave it to Belinda. A business card. "This is a friend of mine. He may be able to help with Kyle. Just tell him that I referred you."

Belinda eyed him suspiciously. She was about to ask how exactly this "friend" of his could help when Stellan stood up straight and gazed out near the shed. Jarrett skulked near the tree line of their properties, looking a little beat up.

"Do you want me to go deal with him?" Stellan said.

"I can deal with Jarrett." Belinda felt along the edge of the business card, wondering how this private investigator would help. "Thanks for the assistance."

Cliffhanger

If Jarrett's nose could talk, it would have a whale of a story and a laundry list of complaints. Jarrett squeezed his nostrils together, holding his head back to stop the blood pouring out of his nose. She'd caught him trying to sneak onto his property via hers, probably to avoid his mom. Belinda had already asked him what happened, and gotten some mumbled reply about a fight with a band member. She wasn't sure if she could believe him or not. Lily came to mind and what he'd been doing with her. She couldn't picture Lily beating him up, but maybe there was someone else involved.

He'd taken off his shoes, but not before leaving a defined mud print in the foyer. The shape and pattern looked just like the one she found before by the side door.

"Do you take that cut through a lot?" Belinda said.

Jarrett rolled his eyes to the side to see her. "I know it's technically trespassing—"

"I'm not so concerned with that, but I am concerned that it looks like you may have been in my house—when I wasn't." Belinda folded her arms.

Jarrett slowly brought his head back down, keeping his now wide eyes on Belinda. "Are you gonna call the police?"

"That depends."

"On what?"

"On whether you tell me why you were here and what you were doing."

Jarrett exhaled loudly. "I just wanted to check on you."

"So you came in even though no one answered?"

"You've had some—incidents—lately. I was worried you couldn't answer."

"That's very sweet of you, but there's a little matter of a lump of money you were carrying around in your backpack too." Belinda got closer, at eye level with him sitting on the counter. "It didn't look like the kind of cash you would just happen to have on you. I know you're waiting tables down on one of the wharves."

Jarrett swallowed. "My parents. I got it from my parents."

"They're generous." Belinda tried to make eye contact with him, but he refused to oblige her.

"Yes, they are." Jarrett jumped off the countertop. "I should get rolling."

Belinda's eyes widened innocently. "So soon? Your nose is still looking a little nasty."

Jarrett laughed nervously. "It's stopped bleeding."

"Make sure to clean yourself up before your mom sees you."

Jarrett nodded, opening the side door.

"And Jarrett."

He stopped and turned.

"Be careful with Lily," Belinda said. "She can be...conniving."

Shock shot through Jarrett's blue eyes and he quickly turned and left. Belinda mulled over the mud print. Jarrett had been inside after Kyle's arrest but before the circuit board fire and she already knew that he could break into their house without leaving obvious signs.

"What do you think he was really doing here?" Victoria returned from the shadows.

Belinda kept her eyes where he'd been sitting. "Let's check and see if anything's missing."

"But you don't think he took anything, do you?"

"I wish I did." Belinda glanced at Victoria sadly. "I think he did something."

~ * ~

Cliffhanger

Bennett and Jonas met them at Victoria's that night. Victoria grinned at Bennett in his newsboy cap and Belinda couldn't stop from smiling herself. Victoria mouthed, "It's so cute!" behind his back and Belinda nodded emphatically. Hadn't she told Victoria earlier? After saying his hellos and chitchatting for a few minutes, Dan vanished upstairs and they didn't see him again. Victoria sat in their circle, all too eager to hear what was going on. She sliced up a tiramisu in the middle of the table, dishing it out to each of them.

Belinda was nervous about how Bennett would treat her after their cold parting, but his eyes softened when she appeared behind Victoria, and her heart relaxed. Maybe he didn't hate her after all.

"I like your friends," Jonas said to Belinda, piling his spoon with the layers of coffee-soaked cake and mascarpone. "I wish Bennett had met you sooner."

"I do serve up a mean store bought cake," Victoria said.

"We should take it upstairs and gather around on your bed," Belinda said with her mouth full.

Victoria snickered. "Invade Dan's sanctuary? That would make for an interesting night."

Bennett watched Belinda curiously as she laughed at Victoria's remark, barely touching his cake. Jonas had already scarfed down his first piece and started on a second. Though Belinda was getting all too used to Bennett's intensity, tonight it made her self-conscious. Residual effects of their argument, she guessed.

"Why not?" Belinda said. "It would be good for him."

"Why would you say that?" Bennett said.

Belinda snickered. "He needs to be bombarded by people now and again. Keeps him on his toes."

"Like you, Bennett," Jonas said, grinning when his friend's steel eyes locked on him. "So, Stellan's news is a game changer."

Belinda and Victoria lit up.

"I can't say Stellan's reasoning for withholding that information makes sense to me," he pushed his plate aside and folded his hands on the floral tablecloth, "but they were just out of high school and dabbling in something they shouldn't have been."

"Still are," Belinda muttered.

"We don't have a way to verify anything he's said so far," Jonas said, eyeing Bennett quickly, "but honestly it sounds more realistic than a seasoned sailor just dying randomly on a perfectly nice day." Jonas rubbed his forehead. "It would be nice if the files on the sailing accident were a little more extensive."

"They're not?" Belinda said.

"It was considered a pretty straightforward accident, which between us, I think had something to do with their families." He sighed. Belinda glanced at Bennett. Maybe he was right. Maybe some of them were baboons. "We could use that boat."

Belinda perked up. "My brother inherited it."

"We know," Jonas said forlornly. "But it's not where your brother says it should be, and there's no trace of it anywhere else."

Belinda looked puzzled, distress coloring her features. Victoria shook her head sympathetically, taking Belinda's hand.

"Belinda," Jonas said, "where was your brother the day of the accident? Really?"

What did he mean by really? Belinda switched from twirling her napkin to shredding it systematically while Bennett watched her in fascination. She didn't want to cry. Not again with Bennett sitting right next to her, but all the secrecy was starting to get to her.

Belinda looked to Victoria and they stared at each other making subtle eye and head movements for a few seconds. Jonas and Bennett just looked on, glancing at each other sideways once in a while to see if the other had any clue about what they were doing.

Somehow Belinda and Victoria established what to do in their non-conversation and they both finally acknowledged Bennett and Jonas again.

"Kyle and Mark planned to sail around the world. They were mapping it out that summer..." Belinda's eyes turned dreamy the way they had on the Ocean Walk. "Bennett, you asked me once if I had good memories of Portside. Those are good memories. Mark spent a ton of time at our house that summer and he and Kyle would spread their navigational charts all over the living room floor. Dad would grill burgers and we'd all just sit outside for hours talking about where they'd go."

Victoria nodded soberly. "They made a good team."

"Kyle and Mark met with a potential sponsor for their around-the-world trip." Belinda tried to not think about it as she talked to stay detached. So far, it was working. "They had planned to do this since elementary school, but Lily had fought to get Mark to do what she was doing—go to law school."

"Mark didn't love the idea and they argued a lot," Victoria said. "People were whispering that their relationship was on the tipping point."

Belinda lowered her eyes. Now came the really not-so-fun part of the story. "A rumor started going around that Mark and I were...involved. With each other." Belinda didn't dare raise her eyes from the table. It was bad enough feeling Bennett watching her, never mind seeing those intense peepers of his.

Victoria picked up the story. "It caused a massive hullabaloo in our circle."

Jonas arched an eyebrow. "What does this have to do with the previous sailing sponsor story exactly?"

Belinda sighed dramatically, still keeping her eyes on the tablecloth. It was a little annoying that neither of them knew anything about these people. "Lily's father happened to be good friends with the potential sponsor, and subsequently decimated their chances of winning him over.

"Mark and Kyle fought about it, and that's why Kyle didn't go with them that day. They were still mad at each other."

"Did Kyle think Mark had something to do with the rumor?" Jonas said.

"No." Belinda heard her voice give and stopped to take a drink. "They were both just frustrated."

Jonas glanced at Bennett, but his eyes were glued to Fawn Eyes.

"Anyway," Belinda said, hoping to switch topics, "I think their fight was the last time they spoke, and that's why Kyle feels so guilty. It's why he doesn't sail; it's why he's let *Sea Stud* rot in stor—" Belinda felt like she'd been hit by lightening. "—age. Storage." She sipped more water, hoping to finish the conversation fast. Why hadn't she thought of it before? If Kyle was going to hide, it made perfect sense. Perfect. Sense.

Belinda smiled at the detective, eyeing her suspiciously, and shrugged. That was the end of her story. Or what she was telling for the night.

She knew where Kyle was.

Chapter 17

The stories about Mark bothered Bennett. He didn't want to feel jealous of a guy who had been dead for close to a decade, but he did. Belinda kept avoiding the subject of Mark and her, bringing it up only in terms of hints and allegations. She obviously didn't want to talk about it, but that bothered him even more.

He'd been staring at the footage from Mr. Trebor's security camera since he got home and it was almost midnight. His eyes blurred over but he kept blinking and rubbing them to stay focused. Maybe the video footage was the wrong track. He thought of the blood smear on the monitor screen at Trebor's shop though. Bennett could feel Trebor was pointing at something on that screen. Maybe what Bennett was looking for was way in the background.

Bennett rewound again to before the accident, zooming to put the background in the foreground, instead of just staring at the car smashing into Trebor's shop. Without that distraction, it was easier to see what else was going on at the same time. He could make out people walking on the other side of the divided road, and then a woman briefly came into view from behind a tree. She looked like she was doing something on her phone. Bennett rewound and watched again. The woman turned, facing the direction of the accident, her phone aimed at Victoria's car as it crashed.

Curious, Bennett zoomed in more. The woman wore sunglasses and the image blurred when he zoomed and she was half-hidden by the tree. But he still felt certain he knew who it was. Bennett grabbed his car keys and sped back to Victoria's house.

The husband answered the door with Victoria right behind him, tying her robe. Bennett apologized, quickly explaining that he thought he'd found something and he needed to see Belinda. Victoria ran upstairs, returning a minute later in just as much of a rush.

"She's gone!" Victoria dug through her purse in a panic.

"What are you doing?" Bennett said, thinking it was exactly the type of thing Belinda would do in a moment of crisis.

"Looking for my cell to call her."

Her husband calmly handed her one of the wireless phones in the house. Victoria grabbed it from his hands and dialed. Bennett watched nonplussed. Where would Belinda have gone in the middle of the night, and without telling them? Victoria hung up far too quickly. "Straight to voicemail."

"You had no idea she left?" Bennett said.

"You think I'm pretend panicking?"

"No, but—"

"I bet she's gone to look for Kyle," Dan said.

Victoria glanced at him sideways. "At midnight? Where would she go to look for him at midnight?"

"How about their family's boat?"

Victoria blanched. "When exactly did this occur to you?"

Dan shrugged. "Right away I think."

Victoria looked like she wanted to punch him. "Why haven't you said anything?"

"It's their boat. I figured she already thought of it."

Victoria threw her arms up in the air. "Kyle is missing! Could you not have just mentioned it in case it slipped Belinda's mind with all the chaos?"

This was amusing and all, but Bennett didn't have time to detour with a marital spat. "Can you tell me where this boat is?"

Victoria gave him the marina and possible slip number, making Bennett swear on his life to make Belinda call her or to call the police if he couldn't find her. He could hear Victoria ranting about "just saying

Cliffhanger

things anyway" as he dashed back to his truck. Bennett grinned. No more sleep for that guy tonight. And none for him either if Belinda wasn't at their boat.

~ * ~

Belinda crept onto the boat, seeing by the light of a streetlamp and a lot of squinting. She'd finally made it to the marina after spending close to thirty minutes hunting for the other set of keys in their house. The boat was pitch black inside and certainly looked empty enough. She tiptoed through the main part of the cabin, every little noise she made amplified in the quiet. Holding her flashlight with the handle out, she went down the stairs toward the staterooms. Empty.

Belinda's heart sank. She was so sure Kyle would be here. Maybe...maybe he had gone to Rio. Or somewhere else far away.

Belinda padded back up. Before she hit the landing, a shadow outside on deck caught her eye. It moved toward the doors, the face just a silhouette. Belinda slid back to the staterooms and hid in the shadows.

Belinda's breathing intensified, gripping her flashlight. She flattened her body against the wall next to the door. Maybe she could pull off some stunt and run out when he came in the room. Probably not, but it sounded good. Belinda steeled herself for the right moment as the person came down the stairs.

She psyched herself up and as he took another step forward, Belinda swung the flashlight across her body as hard as she could, nailing the intruder right in the forehead. He yelled and staggered, his hands flying to the wound.

"What was that?!"

Belinda's eyes popped open. "Kyle!"

"Who did you think it was?"

Belinda dropped the flashlight and threw her arms around him, toppling them both to the floor.

"Okay, okay. Enough!" he said, half-laughing as Belinda kissed his head over and over and practically strangled him.

She let him go, her eyes flashing. "You big jerk!"

"Ow!"

Belinda pummeled his chest with her hands. "I assumed you were dead!"

Kyle curled into a protective ball on the floor as she slapped him. "You know what the first three letters of the word assume are."

Belinda narrowed her eyes. "You vanished! Your Jeep is abandoned in the middle of town. The police think you're in Rio. What was I supposed to think?"

"That...I...went...to...Rio?"

She slapped him again.

"Maybe I should have," he muttered as she bonked him over the head with a pillow. "I kind of had this crazy idea that you'd be glad to see me."

"I am!" she said, whacking him across the face, feathers flying out around them.

She panted and huffed and paced, whacking him a couple of more times for good measure. When he figured he was somewhat safe, Kyle unfurled and stood up. "Do you want to know what happened now?"

Belinda nodded, walking away, and returned with a bandage for his forehead. They stomped up to the galley and Kyle scooped chocolate ice cream into two bowls and slid one across to Belinda. Food always pacified her. Always. She noticed his bowl contained about half the ice cream container and switched her bowl out for that one.

"Hey!" Kyle said, his face drooping.

"I'm having the worst week ever and I want more than that pathetic scoop."

Kyle pulled out the ice cream container to fill up the other bowl and circled his arms around it protectively while he ate. They sat like they had after Belinda got home from Stellan's party.

"What took you so long?" Kyle said, dismayed. "I was giving up officially as of tomorrow."

Belinda shut her eyes, shaking her head in disgust at herself. "It never crossed my mind until tonight."

"Well, no. You were too busy picking out my tombstone."

Belinda glowered. "You act like that made me happy. It did not make me happy. I ugly cried on Bennett's shirt."

Kyle smirked. "Look at it this way: you've gotten to spend more time with him greatly due to me."

"Take the credit all you like. You will anyway." Belinda twirled her spoon in the air. "Why are you hiding here? Why didn't you take your Jeep?"

"The last question is answered by the first question."

Belinda just stared at him and pointed at the clock.

"All right, all right." Kyle inhaled for a dramatic pause.

Belinda dropped her spoon into the empty bowl so it clanged and pushed it away from her. "Drama. Queen."

Kyle shrugged. "I've been hiding, you thought I was dead, the police think I'm in Rio. This is kind of exciting."

"Yes, it was extraordinarily exciting to tell Mom over the phone that you were missing."

Kyle paled to Belinda's satisfaction. "You told Mom and Dad I was missing?"

"And you were scared of them discovering the dead tomato plants." It was nice to know that telling their parents was still a valid threat.

"You said we didn't have to tell them about the car accident."

"Kyle, you knew where I was after that, and I was alive and functioning. You've been missing for three days. I kind of thought our parents should know about that."

Kyle groaned and stuffed more ice cream in his mouth.

"It'll be fine," Belinda said. "You'll talk to them tomorrow. But first, you better start talking to me." Belinda folded her arms on the counter.

"I've kind of been following you around," Kyle said.

"That much I knew."

Kyle arched his eyebrows, the bandage on his forehead scrunching up.

"Bennett figured it out. Continue."

Kyle shrugged. "Well, I'd been doing great until the museum. Someone caught me snooping around and I had to run for it."

"Who?"

"I don't know for sure; I was too busy running for my life. The dude looked like a line backer."

Belinda wrinkled her nose. "Okay, well, why were you following me in the first place?"

"Because somebody else has been following you...for a while."

"The photos." So maybe whoever took those was still playing paparazzi.

"Huh?"

Belinda quickly explained about the photos she found at Lily's, and Bennett's surveillance theory.

"He's right." Kyle folded his arms. "Way back when, one day when you and Mark were out on his boat alone, I saw someone on shore taking photographs. He was trying to look like an innocent tourist, but something was off so I started keeping an eye on you. Sure enough, the same dude kept reappearing in similar circumstances, with a camera."

Cliffhanger

Kyle traced the grain of the countertop. "I blamed Jeff 'cause, you know, he'd been in love with you forever."

"But?"

Kyle's cheekbones tightened. "I bumped into Jeff at the cemetery where Mark's buried right after he got here."

"The fight someone saw."

"Yeah, it started that way. But Jeff wouldn't let me just take off. He calmed me down when he said he was worried about you being back in Portside and wanted me to know that someone had been stalking you the summer Mark died. Turns out, Jeff had been doing the same thing as me. He'd seen someone following you and Mark."

Belinda swallowed. "So, it wasn't Jeff? Ever?"

"Well...I don't know about that. But now I do think he was trying to protect you, even if he was a bit misguided, and I'm worried he figured out who was behind it and that's why he died."

"But...you fought with him." She pointed to his arm with the gash.

Kyle shrugged. "We faked it. We agreed that whoever was behind the stalking was there that night and we were both paranoid and decided to pretend to get into a fight." Kyle's eyes wandered to the cut. "Of course, that sort of backfired on me."

Belinda sat back down. "That basically leaves one person who I can think of who would want to stalk me."

Kyle grimaced. "Loco Lily."

Belinda leaned on the oval island. She could barely make out details of Kyle's face because they'd left the lights off to not draw attention. "I think the reason he died may be more than just because he caught someone following us." She explained Stellan's reveal, watching Kyle's face deepen into a scowl.

"Figures," he said, huffing. "Selfish..." Kyle's mouth formed a hard line.

Belinda was glad her features were hidden in the shadows. After a few minutes of looking menacing, Kyle sighed and shrugged, muttering something about how it was too late now.

"You know it was dangerous just walking in here," he said more cheerfully. "I could have been naked."

Belinda rolled her eyes. "Your missing boat is a bigger concern right now."

Kyle frowned. "The police probably think I'm lying about that too."

"Are you?" Belinda asked sadly. She felt better knowing Kyle had been trying to protect her, but she wished he'd told her what was going on a long time ago. It might have made things easier. Or even safer for them both on some level.

Kyle leaned back, observing her from a distance. "I'm sorry to put you through all of this, Bels. You put up with me, you always have, and you even pretend like you like me."

"Sometimes."

"Sometimes." He gave her a crooked smile. "But you're my constant, you know? And I'm glad you've been here through all of this."

"Me too." Belinda sighed. "The police probably do think you're lying about Mark's boat, which is why we need to find it."

"Bels, I did lie to the police."

Belinda blanched. "About not knowing about the boat?"

"No. Well, not exactly. About the day Mark died. I told that detective that I wasn't there because our grandmother died."

Belinda paused. "Which one?"

Kyle looked up at the ceiling. "I didn't think that far."

Belinda humphed. Well that explained why Jonas asked her the real reason why Kyle wasn't around when Mark died. "Russell Carmichael will be devastated."

"Carmichael? He's still alive?"

"And chasing Nana."

Kyle guffawed. "I bet she makes his life interesting."

"You have no idea. But he keeps coming back for more." She picked up a stray napkin on the counter and started twisting it. "So now that we know Mark was already dead before the supposed accident, we definitely need to find the boat. When was the last time you saw it?"

Kyle thought about it. "Not long after I put it in storage. You know how I was at that point. I couldn't stand the sight of it."

"Who would have known where you kept it?"

Kyle raised his eyes to the ceiling. "Anyone, I guess. I didn't try to keep it a secret."

"Where was it? Was it locked up?"

Kyle shrugged. "It wasn't like I had Bennett Tate guarding the place. I didn't think it was that big of a deal at the time."

Belinda sighed, her eyes watering up. The boat could answer so many questions. About Jeff's murder, of course, but especially all the questions she'd had about Mark for so long.

Kyle pursed his lips. "New topic. I saw you packed up the hutch."

Belinda blinked back her tears. "I see you didn't pack up your stuff."

Kyle flashed his naughty-and-I-know-it smile. "Oops."

"Yeah, big oops when the demolition guys show up to rip up the carpet and find your dirty underwear on the floor."

"I do not keep dirty underwear on the floor."

"How would you know? There could be some hidden under all of your other clothes."

"For your information, I know exactly where everything is."

"That must be why you can't find your wallet on a weekly basis."

Kyle snorted. "You have an unfair advantage in this argument."

"Because I know you so well?"

"Because we shared a crib once and you know how to mind meld."

Belinda grinned. "And yet, I still can't control you."

"You've never really tried." Kyle stroked his chin absently. "Bar glasses."

Belinda glanced back at him, resisting the urge to run home to pack. "Excuse me?"

"You've been stressing over the wedding shower present thing, so that's my two cents. Bar glasses."

"Like the ones Mom and Dad own?"

"Yeah, like those."

Impressive. "That's not a half-bad idea, bro."

"I am good for something."

She smiled. "You're good for a lot of things."

Kyle straightened up, putting a finger to his lips as she was about to say something else. Belinda held perfectly still. They had a visitor.

Chapter 18

Belinda panicked as the boat most definitely rocked. Had someone followed her there? She'd been careful and walked from a good distance to the marina, but if she had a stalker who was not Jeff and not dead then...

Kyle whipped open the door, shining the flashlight right in Bennett's eyes. Bennett faltered backward and toward the edge of the swim platform, losing his balance and half-falling, half-hopping into the water. Kyle caught him by his jacket and dragged him up and onto the boat, helping him to his feet, and looked back into the darkness. "Octopus warthog."

Bennett's eyebrows shot up. "What?"

Belinda appeared in the doorway, thrilled and relieved to see it was Bennett. "It's a twin thing. We have a safe and danger word code system."

"So w–what would y–you have said if she was in t–trouble?"

Kyle cupped his hands around his mouth. "Run!"

Belinda took Bennett's hand, leading him inside where it was warmer. If she wanted him to get over his biases and date her, she couldn't lose him to hypothermia because of her brother and his stupid flashlight. "Are you all right?"

"I c–can o–only see w–white dots," he stammered out after his ice water bath, "but o–other than that I'm just g–great."

Belinda snatched a towel out of Kyle's hands and started patting down Bennett's face and head. He was even hotter when he was wet. "So, Kyle's here."

Bennett smiled wryly. "I g–got that p–part."

"And Bels is here, and now you're here." Kyle folded his arms. "Anybody else coming that you know of?"

Belinda shot him a look. "What are you doing here?"

"I went to see you at V–Victoria's, but you were gone, and her h–husband thought you'd be h–here." Bennett looked around, taking in what he could in the dark. "You k–know, when D–Dan said 'boat,' I had s–something a tad s–smaller pop into my h–head."

Belinda stood back, ignoring for the moment that Bennett had been searching for her. She would savor that and analyze what it meant later. "Dan thought of the boat? Just like that?"

"Great," Kyle snarled. "So Dan thinks of the boat, but it takes you a week."

"Kyle, it did not take me a week. Honestly, I didn't think it would be back from the Caribbean or wherever they sent it this winter yet."

"But I'm not on *that* one, I'm on *this* one."

"Well, I forgot about this one. Temporarily. Anyway," Belinda turned back to Bennett, his eyes darting between the two of them curiously. "Dan thought of this?" Questions painted his face, but he would have to wait to get the scoop on the boats after this was over.

"You can join Victoria in reaming the poor guy out for it later, but I came to warn you that I may know who's behind your assaults." Heat started to reenter his body, especially with Belinda wrapping him up in the towel. It was like being wrapped up in a pelt, and it smelled faintly like the beach, the way Belinda did.

Belinda glanced at Kyle. "Lily Devore?" she said sheepishly.

Bennett rubbed his eyes. "Please tell me I did not just lose my eyesight for nothing."

Belinda got closer to him, examining both of his eyes rimmed with dark circles. She almost reached up and traced the bone underneath, but held back. "What did you find?"

Cliffhanger

Bennett explained what he saw on Trebor's footage, and how he thought it was Lily watching the accident. Possibly even recording it with her phone. Belinda and Kyle looked at each other somberly.

"It's common knowledge she hates your guts," Kyle said, but there was no humor in his voice.

"She certainly made that plain at the museum." Belinda knew Lily was crazy, but this was taking it to a whole new level.

Bennett nodded. "Lily did say you two had unfinished business."

"Meaning she hasn't killed me yet?"

Kyle snorted. "I wouldn't be shocked, would you?"

"All right," Bennett said, folding the towel and handing it back to Belinda. "I'll call Jonas first thing tomorrow." He turned toward the door.

"Are you leaving already?" Belinda blinked her doe eyes at him. "There's safety in numbers."

"You are safe." He glanced at Kyle.

"Not me. You." She wasn't the one about to walk out into the darkness alone.

"Me?" Bennett almost laughed, but her face was so serious.

"Kyle's in all this trouble because of me, why not you? I think you should stay here tonight with us."

Bennett arched his eyebrows. She didn't make it sound like a suggestion.

"He's not sleeping with me," Kyle said.

Belinda rolled her eyes. "We can each have our own stateroom, Kyle. Honestly." She didn't wait for Bennett to agree or seem remotely interested in his opinion, but walked to the landing in front of the stairs and stared at him. "Well, come on. The rooms are down here. Kyle will get you some dry clothes." She looked at Kyle to make sure he heard her command and trotted away.

Kyle smirked at Bennett. "Welcome to my world."

~ * ~

Belinda heard talking and thought it must be Victoria and Dan. But then it sounded like two Dans. Er, two men. Kyle...Kyle and Bennett. Kyle and Bennett! Belinda's eyes opened with a start. It was light out. Sort of. She checked the clock and buried back under the covers until she heard a rap on her door. She didn't answer, hoping he would just go away, but then the door clicked open.

"I could be naked," she grumbled from under the comforter.

"Want me to go get Bennett?"

Belinda glared though she couldn't see him through the fabric.

"I don't like being up this early either," Kyle said, "but we need to leave before it gets later and people show up for work, etcetera."

Belinda peeked out of her cocoon. "We're leaving?"

Belinda dressed and met the two guys in the main deck living area. It felt weird to have actual light after being in the dark for so long. She wandered over, not feeling even close to awake. She'd managed to get dressed and put her hair up, but she wasn't so sure she could communicate yet. Her only real thoughts involved coffee.

Bennett handed Belinda his computer tablet without even saying good morning. "Now about this extra guest at Stellan's party. Look through those photos and see if anyone's a match."

Oh, wonderful. He was a morning person. Belinda stared at the faces for an absurd amount of time before any of them registered, and handed the tablet back to him. "He's not there." She flopped onto the couch. If they weren't getting coffee, she wasn't holding her own weight yet.

Kyle glanced from Belinda to Bennett. "Who are we talking about?"

"I saw a guy posing as a security worker at the party."

"We don't know that," Bennett said.

"I do."

Bennett's eyes glimmered.

Belinda turned to Kyle. "He was a beefy guy with a cue ball head and a big nose."

"Wait, wait, wait," Kyle said, planting his palms on the counter. "Kind of short but stocky? Not a lick of hair."

Belinda nodded.

Kyle snapped his fingers. "That's your stalker."

Belinda and Bennett exchanged looks. His mind was cranking. She could see it. And so was hers, but it was moving in a completely random direction.

"Weimaraners!" she blurted out, then wanted to sink through the floor. She would pay for that by having to explain.

Bennett just looked at her quizzically. "Is that relevant to something we were talking about?"

Belinda flushed. "Oh, no. It's just those funny little dogs that are famous now. Well, I guess they're not really *little* dogs, but, you know..." Bennett's quizzical expression deepened. "I just remembered their name is all. It's one of those things...I couldn't think of the name the other day and it keeps bugging me." She shrugged, hoping to look indifferent. "Now it won't because I remembered." Maybe she should just open the oven door and crawl inside.

"Do you like them? Weimaraners."

"No, not particularly."

Bennett's eyes lightened. "Do things you don't particularly like usually bug you?"

Belinda caught Kyle's smirk from the corner of her eye. "Um...sometimes." Bennett's lip turned up. Well, at least she was amusing him. "Something reminded me of them and it's just annoying when you can't remember."

Bennett seemed satisfied with that and moved on. "So I'll plan to meet up with Jonas today, and the two of you lie low at home."

Belinda nodded at Bennett's advice, so relieved she escaped having to admit to Bennett that the color of his eyes sometimes reminded her of the dogs. "You think we should keep Kyle's reappearance quiet?" Belinda glanced from Bennett to Kyle, his face wrinkled up in thought.

"Yes, I do."

Kyle folded his arms. "I agree. It could be a tactical advantage for us."

Belinda sighed. "Can we eat first?"

Kyle laughed, his eyes brightening. "Catch a murderer or eat breakfast? Bels' chooses breakfast."

Belinda punched his arm, but she was happy to hear him laugh. "If you're going to drag me from my cozy bed at this hour, you're going to feed me, okay?"

Kyle opened his mouth to say something, but Belinda cut him off. "Do you prefer French toast or pancakes?" Belinda said to Bennett. He raised his eyebrows. "We have the stuff to make either so it's up to you."

Bennett nodded. "I like pancakes."

"Pancakes it is then." Belinda flashed a smile. Then her eyes darkened as they settled on Kyle. "You are calling Mom and Dad today." Kyle's mouth gaped. "No. Excuses." Belinda raised her nose up and glided toward the door.

Kyle's eyes held a twinkle as he passed Bennett. "You can't say I didn't warn you."

They split up to hike to their vehicles and return to Belinda's house. Kyle started the engine of her car. He would have to reclaim his

Jeep. There was no way he was taking off alone with her car. "Why didn't I get a vote on what we have for breakfast?"

"Because you're not the guest."

Kyle smirked. "I like how you just glossed over the whole asking him to come over part and skipped right to what he's eating."

"I did ask him."

"Oh, sure. 'Pancakes or French toast?'" Kyle affected a woman's voice, and a poor one at that in Belinda's opinion. "'Pancakes it is, big boy. You're coming over whether you want to or not.'"

Belinda jabbed his shoulder.

"Ow! I'm driving."

"And I'm being hospitable."

"You're holding Bennett hostage and force-feeding him pancakes." She pinched his arm this time, hard. "Ow!"

"Do you think he didn't want to come over?" Belinda wanted to smack her forehead. She never really gave Bennett a chance to say.

Kyle snorted. "He wants to come over. I bet he's been dreaming about your pancakes for days." He grinned wickedly, dodging Belinda's swing at his arm.

"Seriously, Kyle. Do you think he didn't want to come over?"

"Well, I'm not in his head, but I get the feeling he would have just said he wasn't coming over if he didn't want to, so I think you're safe."

"Do you mean that? If you're lying, just come out and say it now and spare yourself the pain later."

"Yes, I mean that. He let you ugly cry on his shirt, he hunted you down when he thought you were in danger, and stayed here last night at your command. There is every indication that he does indeed want to eat your pancakes."

She frowned. "It's too bad he didn't say French toast."

"You could have just rolled with the whole commanding thing you were doing back there and told him he was eating French toast. At our house. Shirtless. Ow!"

Belinda grinned. At Kyle's pain, of course, but she had to admit she didn't mind his last suggestion either. Not. One. Bit.

While Bennett reconvened with Jonas and Kyle hid out at home, Belinda and Victoria detoured a few blocks up from the downtown to shop for a wedding gift. After a lot of eyelash batting and smiling and filling the stomachs of the men in her life with delicious homemade food, she managed to convince her protectors to let her go shop. She was ordered not to leave Victoria's side, and they were to stay in sight of other people at all times. Jonas failed to mention it, but they also had eyes on them.

"Do they have to be crystal?" Victoria said, checking out the price of one glass.

"No, that's just what my parents have." Belinda tried to focus on the glasses, but she kept gazing right through them, her mind a million miles away. "Now so carefully packed away that I don't remember where I put them."

Victoria laughed. "Just don't tell your mom that."

Belinda smirked at the conversation Kyle had had with her parents earlier. She mostly heard "yes, ma'am" and half-finished words on his end. "No worries there. At least they won't be looking for them anytime soon."

"They're too busy getting busy on a cruise."

Belinda made a face. "Unnecessary visual information." Belinda picked up a glass off the shelf, weighing it in her hand. "These are nice."

"Too nice. Look at the tag."

"Oh." Belinda set it back down and moved forward in the aisle. "How hard is it to find bar glasses that aren't chintzy but not extravagant?"

"Pretty hard." Victoria pointed at another shelf with a few more options. Her eyes gleamed as she held a glass under the lights. "These."

Belinda took it from her hand, rolling it over, watching the colors in the glass shift. She met Victoria's eyes and nodded enthusiastically. "They're perfect, Vix. And the price?"

"Perfect."

They gave each other a high five and Belinda admired them while the shop owner wrapped each glass in tissue paper and placed them in a box. The shop door rang and Belinda glanced up to see Lily stalk in. Belinda glanced around, but there was no place to run or hide and Lily was blocking the only exit.

"What are you doing here?" Lily said angrily. Her black hair was pulled back into a tight ponytail. Belinda thought her face would benefit from a more relaxed hairstyle.

Belinda folded her arms. "Buying my cousin a wedding present. You?"

Lily emitted a noise somewhere between a sigh and a snort. "Updating my stemware."

Belinda and Victoria exchanged glances.

"To take back home?" Victoria kept in grabbing distance of Belinda should things get ugly.

Lily examined a nearby champagne flute. "I have a lot to celebrate these days."

"Earning your way to junior partner?" The words came out bitter, somewhat to Belinda's surprise.

Lily's eyes gazed through the flute in her hand. "What would you know about earning anything? All you do is traipse around Portside and throw your name in people's faces."

Belinda seethed. "If you want to know why Mark dumped you, take a good look in the mirror."

Lily turned her piercing eyes on Belinda, her hand clawing at her own throat. "You should've stayed out of it."

Belinda's nostrils flared.

"Well," Victoria said before things got out of hand, "this has been a pleasure as usual." She took Belinda's arm, forcing her toward the door. Belinda hugged the shopping bag, staring Lily down until Victoria practically pushed her outside.

"They have to solve this case before Lily and I kill each other," Belinda hissed, stomping to her car. It was yet another public outburst that everyone would talk about. Well, if nothing else, Belinda was making a splashing re-entry to Portside. "Did you notice how Lily's hand went to her throat? Like she's lost something she keeps forgetting about?"

Victoria returned her credit card to its slot while trying to keep her eye ahead of her. "Maybe. I'm not sure. Like a necklace or something?"

Belinda's pupils dilated. The photos. Lily knew. But how would she have.... Belinda chewed her lip. She should have dug around in Lily's possessions some more. If only she'd had more time. Belinda stepped up her pace, Victoria practically running to keep up.

Belinda zipped them back to one of the main roads to drop Victoria off at the music school. She needed to think and talk to the detective. Not necessarily in that order. If Lily had what Belinda thought she did, then that meant not only did Lily know what had happened on Mark's boat that day, but she also went to his boat—after Belinda left the night before Mark died. That was particularly disturbing after what Stellan had revealed.

Belinda left the glasses in Victoria's care and returned to town, now free to think all she wanted without having to make polite conversation. She reminded herself to thank Kyle for his suggestion. The honeymoon bar glasses were a much better choice than a bread maker. Or ice pick. Especially better than the ice pick.

Chapter 19

"I'm waiting for a warrant to search Lily's house," Jonas said to Bennett. The edge of irritation grew in his voice as he talked. "Mr. Trebor's last noted delivery was to her."

"Quite the puzzler for your first official assignment as leader."

"I keep telling myself it could be worse." He looked longingly at one of the closed bars in downtown as they passed. "How about the mysterious bald stalker?" Jonas detoured across the street, swinging open the coffee shop door. He couldn't drink on duty, but he could pump himself up with legal stimulants.

"Finn and I have crawled through all of the surveillance video that we have and no one who looks like that ever shows up. I'm pretty sure he'd stick out, so I'm guessing if he wasn't meant to be there, he took a back door to avoid being seen by too many people. I only had cameras in the front, first-floor hallways."

"Do you think he knew there'd be cameras?"

Bennett shrugged, scanning the pastry shelves nearby while Jonas ordered some sort of quadruple-infused espresso drink. None of the cakes, scones, or muffins inspired him, though he might feel differently if Belinda offered one to him. When he looked up from his browsing, Belinda was standing right there, her starlight smile lighting up her latte eyes. Not that Bennett was even that crazy about coffee, but the comparison was appropriate considering where they were.

He pulled out his wallet after she ordered, placing the cash in the woman's hand before Belinda could protest. Jonas sipped his beverage across the room, watching the two of them with great interest. Belinda,

Cliffhanger

all grateful and flushed over his financial offering, and Bennett, pleased as punch, even if he didn't look it to a casual observer, to shell out ten dollars on a coffee to see her smile. Jonas had to admit her smile was worth at least that much. He had no problem understanding his friend's growing attraction to the Portside native, and he thought the whole experience was good for Bennett. It was time to get over the past.

After a few seconds, Belinda spotted him and waved, then she and Bennett made their way around the counter to wait for her coffee.

"We were just talking about you," Jonas said, leaning against the high counter.

"I'm sorry to intrude on your gossiping then." Belinda punched a straw into her cup. "Should I worry about what you were saying?"

"Nah. I wouldn't let Bennett say anything bad about you." Jonas winked, enjoying Bennett's glower over top of Belinda's head.

"Well, that's good to know though I'm not sure it's deserved." Belinda grinned, traipsing out of the building where the air was less stuffy. Bennett was right on her heels with Jonas trailing behind him, smirking to himself.

"I ran into Lily today," Belinda looked at Bennett significantly, her nose crinkled up in distaste. "Obnoxious as usual, but I think she's lost something special and I need to know if she had it on at the party."

Bennett scratched his head. "What am I looking for?"

"A necklace."

"Is this significant?" Jonas said.

Belinda glanced at him coyly. "I'll tell you when I find out for myself." Bennett and Jonas exchanged amused glances. "I think the necklace I want Bennett to spy out looks like a knot."

Jonas rubbed his jaw. "This is making me think it's high time I gave the two of you an assignment. You up for some surveillance?"

Belinda lit up. "Seriously? You'd ask me to do that?"

"Don't get too excited," Jonas said. "It's boring work, which is why I'm passing it off to you two." He grinned.

"Who are we supposed to watch?" Bennett said.

"Stellan Mayhew. We may not have pinned him to either death—yet—but he's bound to be guilty of something."

Bennett thought that plopping down on the rocks near Stellan's house under the guise of fishing would be a good way to keep watch, but would be slightly more entertaining to Belinda than sitting in a car waiting for something to happen. So Belinda carpooled in Bennett's truck over to a narrow turnoff on Ocean Avenue. He pulled his fishing pole and bait box out of the back and Belinda followed him across the street to the rocks where she often saw people fishing.

"I had no idea that you liked to fish," Belinda said, balancing her way along the rocks behind Bennett. She held her arms out like a tightrope walker, her eyes glued to her feet as she navigated the path.

"I really don't," he said, having to yell over the waves, "but this is a good spot to watch from."

Belinda nodded, too immersed with not slipping and crashing into the water to make sense of what Bennett said.

Bennett landed on a good, flat spot of rock that was elevated enough to keep them from getting soaked and had Stellan's house in good view. He set his bait box down and held out a hand to help Belinda up. He caught her by her waist as she bobbed around to get her footing, pulling her in closer than he intended. Or, maybe he did intend to pull her in that close. Belinda flushed, loose hairs getting caught in her mouth and eyelashes. At least Bennett's arm prevented her from getting blown off-balance.

Once she had her balance, Bennett let go of her waist, and set the fishing pole in front of her. "Hold this," he commanded while he knelt down to get something out of his box. He came back up with a neon lure with some sort of fuzzy thing attached to one end.

"No worms?" she said, wanting to sigh in relief. She'd been worried about him using live bait. Belinda could just picture him showing up with a bag of live eels and insist that she impale one of them on the hook with her bare hands. And between his steel eyes and clipped sentences, how would she refuse? Especially when they had to stand so close because of the size of the rock.

Bennett's mouth crooked up. "Next time I'll bring something slimy and wriggling just for you."

Belinda made a sour face. "So you don't like to fish, but you do know how apparently."

"My dad loves to fish," he said, holding the hook in front of his eyes as he threaded it through the top of the lure. "I go out with him about once a year. As far as it goes for a pastime, I would say it's too boring. But in this case fishing serves a greater purpose."

"Spying on potential murderers."

Bennett smiled. A tight-lipped smile that could almost pass as a neutral expression, except that Belinda was getting familiar with him and this definitely passed as a smile. For Bennett, anyway. And it was the first time she could say she'd truly seen him smile and witnessing it with her own eyes made her whole day.

"Hold it out," he said.

Belinda looked at him quizzically. "What?"

"The fishing rod." He moved a few paces back so Belinda could face the water head on and indicated for her to swing the line out and drop the lure. Bennett looked around, found a suitable rock to sit on, and helped Belinda maneuver there with the fishing pole in hand.

The rock was cool, even through her jeans, and while it was a relief right then to sit, she knew she would be cursing that unforgiving piece of stone soon enough.

"You watch the fishing line and I'll watch our target."

"What am I watching for?"

"Pull." He tugged on the line.

"It's pulling now though."

"That's just the current. Trust me. You'll know when something's crunching down on it."

Belinda took his word on that and diligently guarded the fishing pole. For a few minutes that is, until she started to feel bored. "Can we talk while we watch?" she said.

"That's your specialty."

Belinda cut him a glance, which he picked up on—and enjoyed—despite her shades. She wiggled around a little to avoid numb butt syndrome and shook her head dismissively.

Bennett handed her a printout of Lily at the party. "Is this what you expected to find?" He pointed to the pendant at the nape of Lily's neck.

Belinda stared at the image and dropped her hand, feeling her stomach constrict. She swung her legs to try and keep cool, but her heart thundered in her chest. She was right about Lily. All this time, she'd known Lily was a rival, but this changed everything.

"Oh!" She jumped from her station. "It's pulling! It's pulling!"

Bennett observed the line calmly. "Well, stop hopping up and down and reel it in."

A couple of old men perched on another set of rocks across from them snickered watching Belinda crank and pull, crank and pull, with Bennett snapping out directions. Belinda yelped as the fish broke the water's surface, flailing and flopping while Bennett got a hold of that end of the line and set him down on the rock. The old men clapped and whistled and Belinda waved back, grinning proudly.

"My first catch!" she said, kneeling down to get a good look. Its iridescent scales sparkled like diamonds in the sunlight, its gills contracting repeatedly and mouth gawking. "Aw, I feel bad now." She

Cliffhanger

examined the hook caught in his jaw.

"Shall I throw him back?" Bennett said, holding the fish down so he could remove the hook. "He's too small to be any use to us anyway." Bennett held the fish firmly then looked back at Belinda. "I think you should do the honors."

Belinda screwed up her face as he stuck the fish out to her, telling her how to hold it so it wouldn't slip away. "Just swing back like you're holding a bat and let him fly."

Belinda nodded, swung her arms back with the fish struggling to escape her hands, and rapidly swung back around. A dazzling rainbow ensued as water flew through the air with the fish, the sunlight reflecting off of its scales, almost blinding them. Belinda laughed as their audience gave her two thumbs up. She went to clap then saw her hands. "Eww," she said, frantically looking for a way to wipe them off.

Bennett ripped a paper towel from his bait box, instructed her to dunk her hands in the salt water near her feet, then thoroughly wiped them down with the towel.

"I smell like fish now." Belinda scrunched her nose up.

"It washes off, I promise."

Belinda smiled as Bennett wiped her final pinky finger of any trace of fish goo, his face intent on his task. For a second, Belinda forgot about the old guys fishing or the cars whirring passed them on the road. All she could feel was the spray as waves crashed in front of them and the tip of her nose as it grew numb and the texture of Bennett's fingers as he held her hand. He raised his eyes to hers and she fell still. Like the water at sunset with maybe a seagull bobbing on the surface.

After a few seconds of gazing at her, Bennett leaned in, and then she leaned in and shut her eyes and was just waiting for his warm lips to meet hers when she felt a sheet of ice water crash over her head. They both froze under the blanket of pin pricks.

Howling laughter from the old men reached their ears. A grin spread across Belinda's face and she got the giggles. To her amazement, it spread to Bennett and they both sat there and laughed. They'd probably just given the older fishermen the best show they'd had in ages.

"I should've brought more paper towels," Bennett said. Belinda giggled, ringing out her sleeve.

"It's a good thing it's sunny." Belinda shimmied back up to the higher rock, raising her face toward the sun.

Bennett joined her, returning to the reason they were actually there, which he temporarily forgot while Belinda's cheeks glowed and her laugh echoed off of the water. Far from being a waste of time, which Bennett never would have thought anyway as long as Belinda was with him, the view of Stellan's house produced results.

Bennett nudged Belinda with his elbow, and she glanced back at him and shrugged after he jutted his head around for no apparent reason. He leaned toward her, whispering for her to look up. She did, trying to be subtle about it. When she turned back to Bennett her face was satisfied if not happy.

Lily Devore half-slid her way back down the path from Stellan's house to her car.

Chapter 20

Belinda and Bennett scurried off the rocks, Bennett half-dragging Belinda along behind him, and jumped into his SUV. Bennett kept Lily's car in sight along Ocean Avenue and onto the main strip into downtown. But Lily cut down a side street and zipped out of sight after a car pulled out in front of them. Bennett muttered to himself while Belinda checked all of the parked cars on the road lined with Colonial-age townhouses in the Historical District.

"Do you think she saw us behind her?" Belinda said. Bennett turned left on the one-way street they finally came to, creeping down the lane. "There! There! That's her car." The silver four-door sat with its tires cockeyed next to the brick sidewalk. "I guess she was in a hurry."

Bennett found a space just down the road, adjusted his mirrors to see the car and scanned their immediate environment for any signs of where she may have gone. "Stay here and keep your eyes on her vehicle. I'm going to see if I can find where she's gone to."

Belinda yanked on his arm. "What if she sees you?"

"I'll be fine, but you keep out of sight." He pointed at her face, his jaw tight. Belinda shrunk back into her seat, her lips plumping into an unintentional pout.

Perfectly kissable lips, he thought as he strolled down the next side street. If he didn't need to worry about following Lily, he would have grabbed her chin and given her the kiss of her life. He loved having her along, but she made it hard for him to concentrate—on his assignment that is. Bennett could focus on her just fine.

Mixed in among the residences was a lawyer, his name on a black plaque engraved with gold near the door. Curious that she was in that vicinity, he picked up the pace, rounding a corner and heading back up the street they'd driven down. Bennett ran his hand over his head. Lily could have gone into downtown for all they knew. This was a convenient—and cheap—place to park. Still, he had a feeling about that other side street with the office. So he circled to go back there, glancing at the truck to check on his associate. His heart stopped when she wasn't in the front seat. Bennett ran over, opening the driver's side and checking the back. No one. He grappled for his phone in his jacket pocket as it vibrated and his heart started beating again. A text. From Belinda.

BG. LILY. PARK.

Bennett didn't know what BG was, but he didn't dare text her back for fear it would ring and draw attention to her. He stretched his mouth into a sharp line and hiked up the hill toward the park, deciding to slip down a side street and come up from the other end. It was only a block long and he would have a good view from there.

He stood on the corner and peered around the building he leaned against, spotting Lily Devore near one of the shade trees, but Bennett couldn't see the man she spoke to. And he couldn't see so much as a hair on Belinda's head. Good girl.

From the way Lily's body was turned, Bennett was afraid she would see him come around the corner and scare them off. Or, more importantly, that he might somehow alert them to Belinda's presence somewhere in the park. So he stayed put, keeping his eye on them and their surroundings.

~ * ~

Lily stood with her arms crossed over her chest and leaned on one leg with her mouth all pinched up while Bald Guy gestured with his hands, apparently doing most of the talking.

Belinda's body was going numb, especially her arm, which she now held up at the elbow with her other hand, recording the entire conversation Bald Guy and Lily were having. She had squeaked into a prime location behind a tree with a trunk like a beer mug, but it was starting to get tough to stand still.

Their conversation was pretty cryptic. Unfortunately, they weren't offering much exposition to explain what they were talking about, though she did hear Jarrett's and Stellan's names more than once. The rendezvous ended with neither participant looking especially thrilled, and Lily went one way while Bald Guy chose another path. Belinda panicked and squished up against the tree as Bald Guy naturally decided to walk in her direction. She held her breath as he passed, thinking she was in the clear when he turned. His round eyes bulged and a vein cutting across his skull protruded as his eyes found her cell phone.

Belinda sprinted but in one step he reached her and clenched her wrist with a hand about five times the size of hers. She wriggled to pry free but he only tightened his grip, twisting her wrist at the same time.

"You keep coming back for more, don't you?" he said.

Belinda wasn't sure what that meant, but she screamed, louder than the pain actually called for, and slammed her foot into his shin. A throb in her foot made it plain that it had hurt her more, but it did distract him and he loosened his grip just enough for her to yank free.

She lost her balance in the process and while Bald Guy tried to get a hold on her ankles, he yelped and doubled over onto his knees. Belinda stood up and backed away as Bennett held the back of an industrial-strength flashlight at Bald Guy's skull.

"Would you like another demonstration on the back of your head?" Bennett said to him, his gray eyes like smoke shooting up from an open fire.

Bald Guy shook his head no.

Within seconds, policemen surrounded the park. Jonas sprinted toward them, his light brown hair whipping up off of his head. Belinda leaned against the tree again, rubbing her wrist, which she was pretty certain was sprained now that she'd collapsed onto it on the ground. Once Bald Guy was in handcuffs, Bennett relaxed his flashlight, but his expression remained leaden. An ambulance pulled up too and Jonas waved them over.

"He's a PI!" Belinda pointed at Bald Guy.

Jonas noted that Bennett had casually (so he thought) moved over to Belinda's side and now stood near her protectively. "He's actually a lawyer," Jonas said.

Belinda's mouth gaped, her finger still pointing. "That's a lawyer?"

"Believe it or not, darling." Jonas planted his feet and looked down at Bald Guy. "Hi."

"Hi back," Bald Guy said.

Jonas grinned. "Assault on a defenseless woman in a park in broad daylight. And it's such beautiful weather too. What is this world coming to?"

Bald Guy grunted.

Belinda watched with interest, unsure if she was more scared or excited by the whole experience. "Do you know him?"

Jonas tilted his head. "Bennett and I had a run-in with him during our private investigating days, didn't we?"

Bald Guy declined to comment.

Belinda's eyes widened. That's why Bennett recognized her description of him. She tried to catch Bennett's eyes, but he stayed fixed on Bald Guy.

"During a case, we found him embroiled in some uncool business practices."

"You never proved it," Bald Guy growled.

Cliffhanger

Jonas shrugged. "You look a little worse than you did the last time we met." He examined the bruise on his jaw—and his earlobe with a clear hole for an earring.

A little bit of pride bubbled up inside of Belinda. Jarrett had put up a fight.

"So what?" Bald Guy said.

"So what?" Belinda stepped right up to him, her brown eyes smoldering. His slits for eyes turned on Belinda. "Don't glare at me, you glorified crook. I can have you disbarred if I want."

Jonas looked back at Bennett. He shrugged.

"There's only one reason someone like Lily Devore would associate with the likes of you, and it's not because of your charming personality."

Bald Guy's scowl diminished.

"I don't care what that plaque on your door reads," Belinda said, hands on hips. "No one on this side of town would hire a lawyer like you. So that means that you're affording an office on that street some other way."

Jonas wanted to clap.

"You should have seen her the other night," Bennett murmured to his friend. "Blows this out of the water."

Bald Guy pressed his lips together tight.

"Don't make me your enemy," Belinda said coldly.

Bald Guy looked up at the disheveled woman with fire in her eyes. She didn't look like much, but something about her told him not to take the warning lightly. "This has been more trouble than it's worth," he grumbled.

"Cooperate with the police," Belinda said, "and I'll consider helping you out in the future."

Bald Guy looked shocked, all his toughness melting from his face.

"I guess someone told you about the path up to the Mayhew house," she said neutrally. "You must be special because that's kind of an inner circle secret."

Bald Guy sniffed.

"Well, you mull over what I've said and decide what your freedom is worth. Because if you don't cooperate," Belinda's eyes turned the color of lava, "you will be on the losing end of this game, proof or not."

Jonas couldn't believe it, but he definitely caught Bald Guy blanch at her statement. And it was a statement. Not a possibility—or even a threat. A statement.

At Jonas' command, the two officers flanking Bald Guy escorted him to one of the police cars and left. Jonas lingered, rubbing his jaw. "Now we come to the part where I ask you what you were thinking."

A paramedic wrapped Belinda's wrist, a mesmerizing experience, so that Bennett had to tap her shoulder to get her attention. "Me? You're asking me?"

"You're the one with the bandage," Jonas said, his green eyes alight with amusement. If Bennett wasn't so besotted with the pixie, he would have asked her out himself.

Belinda looked to Bennett as if searching him for an explanation. "Well," she said, deciding where to start, "Bennett told me to stay in the car while he went to find out what had become of Lily."

"And you obeyed his directions to the letter."

"I intended to." Belinda hopped off the edge of the ambulance, taking Bennett's arm with her non-bandaged one. "But I saw Bald Guy in the side mirror and I couldn't resist following him. Then I saw Lily in the park so I hid quickly and pulled out my phone." She freed herself to get it out, but Bennett held it up and handed it to Jonas. "I got video of their meeting. And sound. I'm positive there's sound."

Jonas pressed play on the screen and held the phone closer to his face to hear. Belinda had quite the steady hand with the camera and he watched the tense exchange between Lily and Bald Guy—as Belinda called Byrne—with interest. "Their conversation doesn't really help us, but this meeting is an interesting turn of events. Byrne, er, Bald Guy, is technically an immigration lawyer with a penchant for moonlighting as an underhanded private investigator. But we do have a common denominator."

"Who?"

"Jeff."

Belinda tucked loose strands of hair behind her ear. They would only blow away again, but she couldn't stop herself from trying. "How is that guy connected to Jeff?"

"You remember the note we found in Jeff's pocket?"

"Yes. It was addressed to Mark. Mark Nichols."

"That is what we guessed. Based on what the note actually said, or what we could get from it after its unfortunate sea bath, I'm guessing now that it was addressed to Bald Guy."

"But his name is Byrne."

"His last name is Byrne. His first name is Mark."

Belinda's memory kicked in. She'd forgotten all about the strange business card that Stellan gave her, and she was ninety-nine percent positive it said Mark Byrne, Private Investigator on it. But she would hold off on saying something just yet. "What did the note say?"

"Something about paying him but he was quitting."

Stellan's shady business deals passed through her mind. "A business deal?"

"Some kind of business, I'm sure."

"You know he was at the party, right?" Belinda said, glancing at Bennett. "Byrne, Mark, Bald Guy. Whatever you want to call him. That was the dude Victoria and I saw in the hallway."

Jonas nodded. "Then we have a few things to talk about. I'm off to deal with him. Keep out of trouble you two." Jonas winked at Bennett.

Belinda examined the bandage on her wrist. She would never be able to wrap it that good. "Are you mad at me?" she said to Bennett.

"Huh?"

"You look mad."

"Not at you." Bennett forced his mouth to turn upwards and took her free hand. "Stop picking at the bandage."

"So what are you thinking?"

"I'm wondering how Byrne is connected. I found his business address scribbled in one of your notebooks."

Belinda thought about the business card in her wallet again. She shrugged and grinned. "It's been a full day, hasn't it?"

"Very full." He looked at her wrist again. "I think it's time to deposit you back home to rest."

"Rest? Humph. Who needs it? I'm just getting started." Belinda took his arm. "Besides, Carmichael's office is not far from here and he might know more about Bald Guy. Plus, he'll want to help me all he can to curry my nana's favor." Belinda smiled wickedly. Bennett agreed that they would pay Carmichael a visit and then Belinda had to go home to rest.

Carmichael welcomed them into his office inside a marine blue townhouse a few streets over from the park. He shooed his secretary away and closed the door on her face as she stood there saying something about how he asked for tea.

"What happened to you, my dear?" Carmichael said, taking her sprained wrist.

"She was assaulted in the park."

"Assaulted?" Carmichael looked from Bennett to Belinda. "Did you call the police?"

"Already taken care of," Belinda said. "I'm okay."

Carmichael held her gaze for a minute until he felt sure she meant it. "Have you had any word on Kyle?"

Belinda shook her head. They'd all agreed it was best to keep his return quiet. "We need your help. Seeing that you're one of the top lawyers in Portside, I thought you'd probably know most of the others in the area."

Belinda could instantly see his feathers start to fluff out. "Who do you want to know about?"

"An immigration lawyer named Mark Byrne," Bennett said.

Carmichael sat back in his seat with his hands on his stomach. "Please tell me you haven't hired him."

"No," Belinda said. "He assaulted me, and he's possibly connected to Jeff."

"That doesn't surprise me as Byrne is definitely connected to Stellan." Carmichael grunted. "He always had to drag that poor boy into his mischief."

Bennett gently pulled Belinda back into her seat as she'd slid to the edge of it.

"Stellan likes his schemes," Carmichael said. "You no doubt heard about different things he was involved in as a kid. Well, it only got worse. I'd heard he hadn't come by all of his money honestly, but it was confirmed when Jeff came to me for advice on how to extract himself from a scheme Stellan had gotten him tangled in. He left out specifics, needless to say, but gave me enough to know it was something very illegal and that Byrne was somehow involved with them."

"When did he come to see you?" Belinda said.

"Right after he got into town apparently. I don't think he wanted anyone to know about it."

"So what did you tell him to do?" Bennett said.

"I advised him to delicately remove himself from the situation, paying them both out if necessary and go back to California and stop answering Stellan's calls."

Belinda thought about her conversation with Jeff at the party. "Did Jeff...did he seem like something else was bothering him?"

"Like what, my dear?"

"Like...like something heavier than that?" Belinda leaned forward. "Murder."

Carmichael blinked through his glasses. "Murder, Belinda? Because of the people he was connected to?"

"No, because of what happened to Mark."

Carmichael processed her statement, saying "oh" several times in different tones. "Jeff was a disturbed young man." He shrugged. "He only opened up about the scheme."

"Thank you."

"It's nothing. And you'll..." Carmichael waved his hand in lieu of finishing the thought.

Belinda smiled knowingly. "I'll be sure to mention this to Nana when I talk to her."

Carmichael smiled.

They left him yelling for his secretary about the tea he'd asked for hours ago. Belinda stared thoughtfully ahead of her as they retraced their steps to the park. If Jeff had tried to extricate himself from the sour business affair and Byrne was also at the party that night...well, it looked like a distinct possibility that Byrne killed him. On the other hand, Jeff had wanted to talk about the sailing accident, which was now confirmed as not an accident, and he seemed absorbed with that, not some crooked alliance. Maybe there was more to Mark's death that Jeff knew that even Stellan didn't realize.

As warned, Bennett immediately drove her home, ordering her to stay put for a while. Yawning, Belinda wasn't feeling like disobeying anyway. At her door, Bennett looked like he wanted to do more than just say good-bye, but he told her he'd see her soon and trailed away. Disappointed again, Belinda watched him drive off and closed the front door.

Chapter 21

The time spent on the rocks confirmed one thing. Well, two actually, from Belinda's perspective. One, someone other than her and Kyle knew about and used the back path up to the Mayhew house. Second, and this was completely unrelated to the case, Bennett was unrelentingly appealing. She never thought she'd see the day she could walk away from fishing and say that she enjoyed it. But wonders never cease and that day had officially come.

Belinda skipped into her home, completely ready to cozy up in her bed with something to munch on, half of her body still damp from their fishing experience, and her heart racing from the afternoon's events.

Kyle met her in the hallway. "Why are you so happy?" She stopped short, realizing she was humming. "You're all wet." Kyle sniffed, making a face. "And you smell like fish. And your wrist is bandaged. What have you been doing?"

"Fishing," Belinda said, her eyes darting to Kyle's hand and what he was holding more importantly.

"Fishing? You?" Kyle laughed. "I know I was checked out for a few days, but did I miss something? Do pigs fly now?"

Belinda put her good hand on her hip. "It wasn't a casual fishing trip if you must know."

"Obviously." Kyle pointed to her wrist. "Was Bennett there?"

"Yes, he was."

Kyle smirked. "So did you catch anything? Other than him of course."

"In fact, I did." Belinda stuck up her nose proudly.

"What kind of fish did you catch?"

"I don't know what it was. Some sort of small, silvery thing." Belinda showed the fish's approximate size with her hands.

"Impressive. So where is it? You probably got one filet, if that, from the sounds of things."

"I told you, it wasn't a casual fishing trip. I threw him back."

"Wait, wait, wait. You touched a live fish?" Kyle tossed his head back and laughed. "Who is this guy? He must have the Book of Belinda hidden away somewhere with all these secrets on how to convince you to do certain things. I sure never could get you to do anything like that."

Belinda narrowed her eyes. "That's because you're my brother."

"Ah, I see. It's because you don't want to make out with me after touching the dead fish." Kyle grinned. "Now about the bandage. Did you slip and fall too?"

Belinda picked at the edges of the bandage until she heard Bennett in her head telling her to cut it out. She tried to explain in brief what she'd done that afternoon, including Bald Guy's arrest.

"It was him spying on you," Kyle said. "It's got to be."

"Bald Guy probably caught you at the museum too. He seems like a real jerk."

"He must be if he's working with Lily."

Her eyes wandered back to what Kyle held. "What do you have there?" She pointed at his hand. Kyle tossed a book in the air, catching it with his other hand and held it out to her. "Our yearbook?"

Kyle smirked. "Your yearbook. I couldn't find mine."

"You went and dug this out? Why?"

"Just curious with everything going on." He shrugged. "I thought you might want to see it too." Belinda smiled, flipping through the pages of the hardcover book. He couldn't find his wallet that morning, but their yearbook.... "Now that you've learned how to fish and gotten over your phobia of slimy things, you can move on to case solving and really blow Bennett Tate's clockwork mind." He dodged her swing with the book and ran into his room, shutting the door before she could strike again.

"I like his clockwork mind," she said through the door and she could hear Kyle chuckle. Belinda sighed and took her book and plopped onto her bed, then groaned when she realized she'd forgotten to change out of her wet clothes.

She flipped through the pages of the book, scanning all of the messages. Most of the notes were bland congratulations with a lot of phone numbers mixed in. She was pretty sure she didn't call half of those people.

Belinda purposely took her time reading them anyway, not wanting to admit to herself whose note she wanted to hurry up and find. Eventually, she came to it. Mark's note was actually just a sketch. A simple doodle of a special knot. Belinda traced the lines. Though she hadn't looked at it in years, Belinda could still see it exactly in her mind. Mark had taught her to tie knots one summer when they were younger and it had become their symbol, almost an inside joke. The thing that had solidified their friendship ages ago.

Then the summer after graduation, that knot became their symbol for a meeting place. Mark knew about this abandoned warehouse that the Mayhews owned. They'd meet up there and sometimes Mark hauled *Sea Stud* into the docks and they'd go out to swim for the afternoon. Belinda had never even told Kyle that she and Mark had met up alone sometimes. But her mind rewound to the photos Lily had of her and Mark on the boat alone. Did Lily know about the warehouse?

She scrambled through her purse, digging out the business card from Stellan. She flipped it over, the address of the supposedly abandoned warehouse written in black ink. Obviously, he hadn't meant to give her that information, but she knew Byrne and Stellan were connected now, and not because of Byrne's private investigating skills, so it was too late. Byrne was now also connected to Lily. She tapped the card against her chin. *Sea Stud* was in that warehouse, she could feel it.

Belinda ran out of her room, bumping into Kyle coming out of his. "Are you all right?" he said. "You look a little wild-eyed."

"No, no." Belinda wanted to rope her heart and pin it to the ground to keep calm. "I just remembered I needed something from the store. I wanna take care of it before I get comfortable." She forced a smile.

Kyle looked her over, still damp, and definitely excited or nervous about something. He watched her suspiciously while he offered her some chocolate candies, which she turned down, and pushed past him down the stairs. The door slammed and Kyle chewed on his candy thoughtfully and went to check out her yearbook.

As Belinda zipped out of her driveway toward the warehouse, an unseen spy left to meet her there.

~ * ~

The warehouse was located on the water outside of Portside. For all intents and purposes it looked abandoned to Belinda, but she knew that Stellan's family had earned their wealth the hard way and that this metal box was once the flourishing headquarters of his family's business. Something fish-related, Belinda thought. How they earned their money had changed over the years, but they apparently still held a soft spot for how it all started. Why else would they keep such an eyesore?

Belinda parked on the edge of the property, scoping out the uneven parking lot before heading toward the warehouse. Whatever life existed outside of the property was hidden by trees and brush. It seemed the sentimentality for the place stopped with just holding onto the property. Belinda wondered if they'd used it for anything in recent history, or at least since Stellan's father died.

She marched toward the main warehouse, which looked like the most promising place to keep a boat. Belinda took a deep breath and slowly twisted the knob of the door on the side of the corrugated metal. She switched on a flashlight, waving it around before stepping all the way inside. Belinda crept along, keeping her eyes and ears alert for any signs of wild creatures taking refuge in the rafters, especially ones with wings.

Once inside, Belinda could see a couple of tables set up with boxes stacked on and around them. Curious, she slowly pulled back one of the box flaps that was loose, prepared for something furry with teeth to jump out at her. But she only found inanimate papers. Official looking. She flipped through a stack, and lifted up one of several little booklets. Visas? Passports? Belinda pursed her lips. Bald Guy was an immigration lawyer. A bird flew around the roof, scaring her to death and she dropped them, pushing the box away.

She picked up speed in a diagonal line from the door, spotting something with her flashlight in the opposite corner toward the back. Sure enough, it was a boat. She ran the flashlight back and forth to find the stern, noticing there was another door on that end. Belinda flung it open to let light and air inside and stood behind the stern to read the name. *Sea Stud.*

Sometimes she felt that the boat became the center of attention in the whole story instead of the people involved. It was the setting for a horrible tragedy, and it stood there now in decay as a sign of how deeply that event had affected certain people. Kyle was just letting it rot, along with his passion for sailing.

Belinda reached her hand out to the stern, touching the peeling letters that spelled Portside under the boat name. She wanted to get onto it, but it was too high up on the pilings to reach the sides and there was no swim platform to grab hold of. She flicked the flashlight back on and reentered the dark warehouse, spotting what looked like a crate. After trying to pull it across the rock-infested pavement while still holding the flashlight, Belinda set the light on top of the box, and made it across to the boat in much better time. She set the light down on the deck, and with her uninjured palm and one leg, pulled her body up and under the railing. She stood up to find her clothes had wiped off all of the dirt build-up on the boat and dusted herself off as good as possible.

She opened the hatch to the cabin, more spacious than you would give a sailboat that size credit for. After scoping out the situation with her flashlight, she took a deep breath and climbed down, a tiny bit scared of what she would find down there besides dirt. The interior had apparently been stripped of anything not native to the boat. Not that you could keep a lot of knickknacks around on a moving craft, but she knew Mark had had some personal touches on board that were now missing.

Belinda leaned against one of the dining table benches. Goodness, she had a lot of memories wrapped up in this piece of fiberglass. So many summer days sailing in the bay and striking out beyond into the straight Atlantic. Anchoring in various alcoves to swim. Curled up in sweatshirts and watching the sun set over the water. Mark kissing her that one time...

And then Belinda's lights went out.

Chapter 22

Jonas flew into Belinda's and Kyle's driveway on his bike, his hair streaked back by the wind. He jumped off, laying his bike on the grass and ran up to the door, trying to catch his breath as he waited. Kyle looked a little surprised to see him, but no matter. He wasn't there for that.

"I need to see Belinda," Jonas huffed. "We know who hired Byrne and what Trebor probably found at Lily's, and she needs protection, right now."

Kyle's eyes, neutral up to that point, flew open and he ran up the stairs, slamming the door in Jonas' face in the process. Jonas rolled his eyes and muttered something about manners. Seconds later, he reappeared, plowing past Jonas into the yard.

"She's gone!" Kyle threw his arms in the air, heading straight for his Jeep.

"To go shopping?"

Kyle looked at him hard. "To go to Stellan's warehouse. She thinks *Sea Stud* is there."

Jonas ran to get in Kyle's Jeep before he took off. Kyle backed up in an L over the grass to turn. Jonas' heart sank as the Jeep bounced up and down, metal crunching under the tires. He glanced sadly behind him as they raced to the end of the driveway.

"Sorry," Kyle murmured and stepped on the gas.

Jonas tried Belinda on her cell every few seconds while they drove. Nothing. Straight to voicemail, which meant it wasn't even on. "This is bad. Bad, bad, bad."

Kyle looked to him in panic. "If you're saying this is bad—"

"Dude, watch the road!"

Cliffhanger

Kyle swerved, nearly running into a sand dune to avoid a runner.

"How did you get your license exactly?"

"Just tell me we'll find my sister."

"We'll find your sister. Now please keep your eyes on the road." Jonas rubbed his forehead. He was getting a migraine. "Why is Belinda so obsessed with the stupid boat?"

Kyle didn't answer, his expression hard.

"Kyle, please. I'm trying to help you. What is the importance of finding *Sea Stud* for her? Besides the sailing...whatever we want to call it now."

"It's not *Sea Stud*. It's Mark."

Jonas licked his lips. "Was she involved with him?"

Kyle hesitated, his eyes glued to the road now. "She doesn't think I know they spent so much time together that summer, but Mark finally confessed and told me his plans to break it off with Lily and start dating my sister. Openly."

Jonas wrapped his mind around that. "So she's doing all of this for emotion...sentiment?"

"I don't know, man. I don't pretend to understand her, all right? But I promise you that's why she's going there. It's all about Mark. All of it." He banged his palm against the steering wheel.

"Were you gone the day he died because you were mad at each other? Because of the failed sponsorship?"

"What? No!" Kyle laughed incredulously. "Is that what Bels told you?" He shook his head. "One sponsor blowing us off because of Lily's father was not that upsetting. I mean, in the long-run it just didn't matter. The Devores always liked to make plays like that against other families to show off I guess, but we knew we'd get another sponsor, probably a better one, within a month or two."

"But you guys fought."

Kyle scratched his head, a smirk in the corner of his mouth. "I'm sure we did, but I think it had more to do with the rumor. Mark was angry that Bels got dragged into it. In any case, I finally told him about the spy following them around." Kyle's eyes grew serious. "I think he knew it too, though he didn't say as much to me."

"Do you think he suspected Lily was behind it?"

Kyle searched the road ahead for answers. "I wouldn't doubt it. She had gotten more jealous and possessive that year. I think she could sense her time was running out."

Jonas called Bennett. They needed all the help they could get.

~ * ~

While still on the phone with Jonas, Bennett hurried into the garage to get in his truck when he saw something that shouldn't have been there. Muddy footprints. Just like at Belinda's. Bennett spun around to find Jarrett.

Bennett grabbed him by the arm before the kid could move and whipped him around in a circle, pinning him to the worktable. Jarrett struggled, breathing heavy and trying to see his assailant.

"What have you done?" Bennett yelled in his face.

Jarrett's deep blue eyes swirled in confusion. "I don't know what you mean."

Bennett tightened his grip.

"I don't know!" Jarrett's voice cracked. "I came to tell you...I'm scared. I...I thought you could help."

He sounded sincere so Bennett loosened his grip a little. "Have you figured out Lily was using you?"

Jarrett nodded. "I'm sorry for what I did. I wasn't thinking straight."

"I'll say. How you thought hurting Belinda—or worse—would endear her to you is beyond me."

"You don't understand. She wasn't supposed to get hurt. Not really. She was supposed to be in trouble and then I...I..."

"You would show up and rescue her?"

Jarrett nodded pathetically. "But you kept getting in my way. First, at the accident you showed up, and then you were there when I wanted to visit her afterward. Then with the fire, that cop showed up before I could get there!"

"Did it never occur to you that what you were doing could have gotten her killed whether you planned to show up to save her or not? Or that perhaps the person suggesting it wanted her to end up dead?"

"I know it was a stupid idea now, but I just wanted her attention. I thought she'd change her mind...see me as an adult if I could help her."

Bennett loosened his grip some more, feeling a little sorry for the kid. He was clearly an idiot, but still.

"Lily suggested it," Jarrett said. "I saw her at the market after you left with Belinda and I thought you were dating and was mad. Lily asked what was wrong...so I told her. And then she said to meet her later because she had some advice for me." Jarrett looked ashamed. "I had no idea she hated Belinda. Or that she wanted to hurt her."

"What tipped you off?" Bennett said sarcastically.

"Look at me, man." Bennett studied the bruises on his face and his bulging lip. "After the fire, I saw Belinda on the stretcher with an oxygen mask and it hit me that what I was doing was crazy, so I told Lily thanks and all, but I was done. Then some bald thug helping her out beat me up, threatening to do worse if I told anyone."

"Did you drive the car that hit Belinda and Victoria?"

"No." Jarrett swallowed. "I just went and paid for it and all. I was nearby when it happened, but it didn't matter. You still got to her first. But I...I did drive past you at the museum. I was just angry and stupid."

Why did people always state the obvious? "I'm well aware that you're stupid. You put the rental under Kyle's name."

"That was Lily's idea, not mine," he said bitterly.

"You didn't refuse."

Jarrett looked down again. "I know."

"You know, you could have killed Victoria's baby. A trauma like that might have caused her to miscarry."

Jarrett tried to nod, blinking furiously. Bennett helped him up, straightening out the kid's jacket. In a strange way, Bennett understood his desperation.

"I just wanted to know why Belinda likes you and not me." Jarrett kept his eyes on the cement floor.

"For one, I'm not trying to get her injured or killed for my personal benefit. And two, she won't be put in jail for dating me."

"I'm eighteen," Jarrett said indignantly.

Bennett shrugged. "Do you want to help save her for real or not? Belinda is missing and more than likely it's because of Lily."

"I'm not sure I can help."

"I wouldn't say that." Bennett slapped the back of his shoulder. "You have childish innocence on your side."

Jarrett glowered.

"You can start thinking of how to make up for your stupidity while I drive," Bennett said. "Get in the truck."

Bennett and Jarrett were already at the warehouse when Kyle drove up. They ran toward them, Bennett waving his hands in the air. Kyle zipped around him, near Belinda's car, slamming on the brakes.

"The boat's gone," Bennett said breathlessly. "But it was definitely here; the pilings are still inside and there are tracks in the dirt."

Kyle swore, slamming his hand on the steering wheel and set off the horn.

Jonas stared calmly at the warehouse, planning their next move. This was his case, and that wonderful woman wasn't disappearing permanently on his watch. Jonas turned to Kyle.

"Is the boat water worthy?" Jonas said.

Kyle looked scared and furious simultaneously. "Last time I saw it. Why?"

"I'm just wondering..." Jonas gazed out past Bennett to the harbor.

Bennett's jaw tightened. "The two other people connected to this case died in the water. And the truck tracks in the warehouse..." Bennett glanced behind him, his eyes drawing a line between the warehouse and the boat ramp.

Jarrett swallowed. "I heard Lily's thug say something about it costing more to put it in the water."

Kyle snapped to attention. "What do you mean? What are you thinking?"

"Get us to the harbor," Jonas said while Bennett climbed over him into the backseat. "You—" Jonas pointed at Jarrett. "Call your parents and tell them what you've done. You'll need a good lawyer, but you get some points with me for helping out here."

The harbormaster waited for them as Kyle screeched to a stop right at the water's edge. Jonas wasn't a squeamish person, but when Kyle finally stopped, he actually let out a huge sigh of relief that they made it there alive—and didn't dive hood first into the harbor.

Jonas and the harbormaster yelled back and forth over the dual outboard engines. They had no way to find *Sea Stud's* position. As they flew out of the harbor, all three men hanging over the sides to keep lookout, Jonas quelled a sudden shot of panic. So much water out there. And they didn't even know for sure that this is what was happening. It was just a hunch.

Jonas took in a huge gulp of salt air. His superior officer told him the day of his promotion that his gut got him the new job. At that moment, he felt the weight of the world riding on that statement. If anything happened to Belinda, this would be his first and last case.

Chapter 23

Belinda could feel the world rocking around her. Movement like a car, but it wasn't a car. It was like being sloshed around...in water. On a boat. She opened her eyes, panicked and relieved at the same moment. Panicked because she was on a boat—*Sea Stud* if she was right—on the water. And relieved because she did wake up, which meant she was alive.

But her relief quickly passed as she came to and felt something sticky and tight on her mouth. Her hands were behind her back, wrapped together. And when she tried to move her legs, her feet were bound. Her impulsive behavior was coming back to bite her. Without meaning to, she heard a whimper escape her taped mouth and tears formed in fear.

A pendant in the shape of a knot encrusted with tiny diamonds descended in front of her face like a spider, swaying from side to side. Lily stepped over Belinda, lying on her side on the floor of the cabin, and kneeled down, tilting her head to the side to look her in the face. Belinda couldn't hide her fear, her eyes wide with it. Lily sneered.

"Not so uppity without a roomful of people to come to your rescue, huh?"

Belinda breathed hard, barely controlling herself from bursting into tears.

"I bet this is the first time in your whole life you can't say a word. So let me set something straight for you." Lily leaned closer, her dark eyes wrathful. "Nobody takes what I want from me. Especially not some spoiled trust fund baby whose pathetic life I can stamp out. Mark learned that the hard way. And so will you."

A tear slipped across Belinda's cheek. Lily wiped it away gently, Belinda recoiling at her touch.

"If you'd only kept your hands to yourself," Lily said, "you wouldn't be here." She stood and Belinda listened to her footsteps trail up to the deck.

Belinda closed her eyes tight, breathing in and out deeply to steady herself. As badly as she wanted to lose it, this was no time to fall apart. If her life ever depended on her sanity, it was right then. What had she been thinking about before she blacked out? Mark. And that first and last time they kissed. What was that day like? It was hard to remember under the circumstances, but Belinda forced herself to recreate it in her mind.

It was August, the end of their fun time as all three of them had to get ready to start college. But nobody was in a rush for that summer to end. The weather had been perfect and Belinda was glad they'd used every spare minute to be on the water. Especially looking back. Kyle was always with them, but that day he'd had something going on, but Mark asked Belinda to go out with him anyway. It was a perfect day to swim so she didn't argue. They stayed out all afternoon and watched the sunset on the Atlantic.

That's when Mark told her...he told her he'd broken up with Lily. That he was going to study engineering, but he and Kyle were going right on ahead with their plans to sail the world. And Mark couldn't wait for the holiday break so they could see each other again. The way he'd said it kind of sounded like he wanted to see them both. But then he'd looked straight at her, his deep blue eyes saying something completely different. His brown hair curled up around his forehead and he'd smiled. Mark didn't have a compartment of smiles like Kyle. He just had that one, but it made her heart gush.

Then he gave her the knot pendant and they'd both laughed because it was a silly thing, but it still meant so much to the both of them. Before she had time to process any of it, Mark kissed her. Soft and hard at once, and Belinda wrapped her arms around him as he brought her closer, inhaling the mixture of sunscreen and salt always emanating from him. They stayed out until twilight, finally forced to separate to get back into the harbor before dark. The last time she saw him was on the dock when he promised he'd call the next night and they'd go out again that coming weekend.

But Mark didn't make it until that weekend.

If she'd only looked harder.... Belinda squeezed her eyes closed. She'd left the necklace on *Sea Stud* by accident, and ran back that night to get it. But Mark wasn't on board. The lights were on in the cabin and his car was in the lot, but he was gone. She couldn't find the necklace and when he didn't show, or answer his phone, she figured he'd run out to get something. They were right in town so he could've walked. But now Belinda knew why he was missing and she wanted so badly to redo that night. He was already dead or dying. Lily knew what had happened that day, and she killed Mark for it.

And now she was going to finally kill Belinda too.

"Well, Belinda," Lily crooned as she reentered the cabin, "the coast, quite literally, is clear, which is unfortunate for you. So I'm afraid it's time."

Lily yanked on Belinda's arms, forcing her up and to her feet. But Belinda's feet were also tied, so Lily grunted and panted, having to pull a reluctant Belinda along who refused to hop or help her in any way. If this Montresor thought Belinda was actually going to make it easy for her to drag Belinda to her own death, she was nuttier than she thought.

Belinda's mind raced as Lily dragged her up the stairs to the deck. She could feel the bruises forming as she clunked along, getting thrown into the sides as the boat rocked. She closed her eyes as full sun hit her. Lily left her on deck, clearly not worried about Belinda escaping. From what she could see, there was no direct hope of that. Nothing but water and sky.

"Mark was pretty surprised to see me that night," Lily said, admiring what looked like a bike chain. "When I told him I knew you two had gotten cozy long before then, he had the audacity to say nothing had happened until he dumped me. Well, I assured him that, even if I did believe him, I didn't care. The two of you would pay for making a fool of me."

Belinda had a pretty good idea of what Lily had in mind now and wriggled around, trying to loosen her wrist bonds. But Lily had spent too much time with Mark. She knew how to tie a knot.

Lily laughed. "Mark warned me to stay away from you, but I told him he wouldn't be around to protect you. Then I cracked his head open before he could stop me. I didn't plan on Stellan being such a coward. Or Jeff spying me leaving Mark's sailboat that night and being smart enough to put it together." Her eyes gazed in the direction of the harbor. "It was supposed to be a murder that you would be blamed for. Ah, well. This works too." Lily pulled the necklace out and slipped it over Belinda's head, fondling the pendant. "I never meant to hold on to this for so long, but I couldn't ever quite let it go." Lily's eyes focused on Belinda's. "I guess it's time."

Lily hoisted Belinda's feet in the air, so Belinda took her chances and kicked her legs as hard as possible. On dry land, it might've only irritated Lily. But this was not dry land. Lily fell backward, crashing near the cabin door. It stunned her because she sat still long enough for Belinda to get up on her knees and try and scuttle as far away as possible. She had no other game plan with her restraints, which felt like they got tighter as she struggled. And the more she saw of her surroundings, the more despairing she became. But she refused to just sit there and cry while Lily murdered her.

Before Belinda could crawl her way to the other side of the boat as waves knocked her off balance, Lily got her footing again and pulled Belinda up. If she thought that would be safer, she was wrong. As soon as Lily bent over to wrap the bike chain around her ankles, Belinda buckled her knees and thrust her body forward, knocking Lily in the face and toppling her over. She yelled as she rolled on the deck, just shy of sliding overboard. Belinda cursed, wishing she could just waltz across and push Lily over, but she was doing good to stay standing.

Then she saw it. The sun glinted off of a moving object in the distance and it was hurtling towards them. Could it be another boat? Could it even be someone she knew? But she didn't have much time to hope. Lily pulled her legs out from under her and Belinda slammed onto the fiberglass, the wind knocked right out of her. She laid there paralyzed, trying to breathe, while Lily wrapped the chain around her ankles.

As soon as air surged into Belinda's lungs again, she swung her feet at Lily's head. But Lily dodged, yanking Belinda to the lower deck. Seeing the water, feeling the metal weighing down her feet sent new shockwaves of fear through her. But also renewed determination. Before Lily could pull her over the edge, Belinda channeled all of her energy, squeezing it through her torso down into her leg muscles, and snapped her legs out.

Lily staggered into the ship's wheel and pushed Belinda off the side with her feet as the boat took a sharp left. She stood taller as Belinda slid into the water screaming, smug and eager to watch her die a slow death. But she'd set things in motion, and as the boat careened sideways into a swell, Lily flew backward. The last thing she saw as her temple drove into the corner of the cabin entrance was the shape of someone who looked like Mark standing on the bow of a motorboat.

~ * ~

Bennett squinted into the sun, his body slung over as far as he could manage without falling out of the boat as spray doused him with every wave they hit. He had one side, Jonas the other, and Kyle the bow. Just then Kyle turned yelling, his words stolen by the wind. He pointed and as the boat swerved, Bennett aimed his binoculars in that direction, adjusting them to see clearer.

Kyle hunched on the prow ready for battle. Bennett ripped his jacket off as Kyle dove off the bow. The harbormaster took a sharp right and Bennett dove from the side. He surfaced, seeing Kyle's and Belinda's heads, but she had tape across her mouth, and she was slipping from Kyle's grip. Bennett fought the current and the waves. It had been a while since his stint as a lifeguard, but he felt the training coming back to him. Kyle ripped the tape from Belinda's mouth, but struggled to keep her above water.

"We've got you," Bennett told Belinda. "You're not going anywhere."

She fought to keep her mouth and nose above water, her breaths shallow. Kyle ordered her to breathe deeper while Bennett dove under, the salt burning his eyes as he tried to see to remove the chain from her legs. In Lily's hurry, she'd just wrapped it with no real knot, but it was still tough to unwind underwater, especially with Belinda flailing her legs. Not moving out of the way in time, one end of the chain flew straight into the side of his head. He surfaced, gripping the lifesaver for support as his head started to throb.

Jonas pulled Belinda on board. She collapsed into his arms, coughing and crying. He lifted her onto a seat while Kyle helped Bennett up, now really feeling the pain in his temple. Kyle and Jonas untied and unchained Belinda, now just crying. Kyle hopped up next to her as she blabbered incomprehensibly.

"Bels, Bels, just...just stop talking right now." Kyle held her tight, his golden brown eyes betraying how scared he really was. By some miracle, his sister obeyed and just cried into his shoulder.

Jonas slapped Bennett on the back as they watched from a respectful distance. "Good job," Bennett said, keeping his eyes on Belinda.

Jonas gazed over at *Sea Stud*—and Lily's still body. "You too."

"It's okay if you're relieved." Bennett swallowed. "It's been an intense case."

"Thank you." Jonas half-smiled. "I may have to cry myself. When I'm home, in the dark, of course."

Belinda got herself together a little more, and slid off the seat with Kyle holding her arm to keep her steady. She was about to say something like thank you, when she realized that was hardly going to express how she felt, so she just flew with her impulse and wrapped her arms around Jonas' neck. It took Jonas a few seconds to recover and hug her back.

"You're starting to feel like an old friend," Belinda said, releasing him. "We're having you over for dinner. No protesting."

Jonas nodded, not even considering the idea of protesting. "I'll bring the beer."

Belinda grinned, meeting Bennett's gaze. Bennett smiled back in his way, and she reached for him and—

"Wait!" Kyle dove between them, putting his hands up. "Wait, wait, wait." He locked eyes with Bennett. "Do you currently have a psychotic girlfriend?"

"Kyle!" Belinda rolled her eyes.

"No," Bennett said solemnly.

"Have you *ever* had a psychotic girlfriend?"

Bennett looked to the sky, giving that a moment's thought. When he didn't answer right away, Belinda started to worry and held her breath.

"No."

She exhaled. "Are you done?"

Kyle thought a minute. "Yep."

"Then please move."

He stepped back and before anyone else could get in the way or object or kidnap her, Belinda threw her arms around Bennett, planting her lips on his at the same moment. Bennett didn't hesitate to respond this time, clutching her back tightly. Jonas arched his eyebrows and Kyle wrinkled his nose.

Belinda pulled away, both of their eyes sparkling. Bennett licked his lips. "Salty."

Chapter 24

Belinda sat between Kyle and Bennett on the boat as they chugged back up through the bay to Portside Harbor. It was such a clear, perfect day that *Sea Stud* was still visible on the horizon as the police worked to deal with the aftermath, namely Lily's dead body.

Belinda wanted to feel sorry that she'd died, but the few horrible seconds she was trapped underwater because of Lily successfully killed any hope of that happening. Not to mention Lily had admitted to killing Mark, and Belinda shivered at what she'd put Jeff through in his final moments alive. No, this was better.

Belinda wrapped the blanket tighter around her shoulders and turned to Bennett. "Did I kick you in the head?"

Bennett held the side of his head, trying to ignore the stabbing pain on the side where the chain had flogged him. His mouth creased almost imperceptibly. "Yes, you did."

"I'm really sorry." Belinda placed her hand on his head gently. "I—"

Bennett placed his fingers on her lips. "You have nothing to apologize for. Nothing."

Belinda relaxed, but kept patting his hair. "Actually, I do. I haven't been completely straight with you. You asked me if I was involved with Mark and I never gave you an honest answer." Belinda inhaled. "We were involved, though not for very long. Technically, we had one official day together, but it started long before that. I...I was embarrassed when you asked. But that's the truth."

Bennett nodded. "Okay."

Belinda bit her lip, working up her courage. "What was her name?"

Bennett seemed to snap out of some reverie, his hair still dripping down the side of his face to his neck. "What *her* are you talking about?"

"Her—the one who biased you against women of fortune."

Bennett licked his lips.

"Come on," Belinda said, slapping his knee with the back of her hand. "It's only fair since you know...you know."

Bennett hesitated, but the look in Belinda's eyes...this could work. Why not just surrender? "Alexa Dupuis."

Belinda's eyes went wide. No wonder he'd gotten jaded. "You went out with her?" she whispered. "Oh, Bennett. No wonder you hate us."

Bennett's eyes glinted. The first time in a while.

"She has issues. Big time." Belinda rolled her eyes. "She did anything and everything to annoy her parents in high school. Whatever she knew they hated, she went after with a vengeance. She went Goth for a semester because it sent her father into a rage just to see her with black nail polish one time. And she never dated anyone for the right reasons. At least, that I know of."

"So you're saying I was one in a long line."

"A very long line."

Bennett's whole face started to turn down.

"No," Belinda said. "No frowny face. You didn't know. And, well, Alexa is awfully pretty and charming when she wants to be. And it happened a while ago, right?"

Bennett nodded slowly, his jaw twitching.

"So, there you go. Hindsight and all that."

"You shouldn't feel bad," Kyle said, squished up next to Belinda in the seat. "Even knowing all of this, the guys in our school were still dumb enough to date her."

Belinda jammed her elbow in his ribs and shushed him.

He rubbed his side. "Why did I want to save you again?"

Bennett's lip curled up on one side. "She's not nearly as pretty or charming now that I've met you."

Belinda's face softened, her doe eyes twinkling. "I hate to toot my own horn, but one of the hottest guys in our class did say once that if he had to choose between us, he would pick me."

"He was also one of the dumbest," Kyle muttered.

Belinda ignored him.

"He had good taste," Bennett said.

"I see where this is going," Kyle said, sliding off the seat, "so I'm just gonna go over here." He slipped to the other side of the boat, leaning over the side. Belinda watched him stick his nose into the wind for a second, then turned back to Bennett.

"So I guess I have to forgive you now," Belinda said. "For insinuating that because I'm rich, I'm a spoiled, rebellious snob who toys with a man's feelings."

Bennett raised his eyebrows. "In that case, I forgive you too."

Belinda whipped her head around. "For what?"

"For making me the least rational I've been in a very long time."

Belinda's snarl instantly spread into a smile. "I'll take that as a compliment."

Then Bennett kissed her, and for once it was a thousand times better than her daydreams. At least.

~ * ~

Belinda stood in her bedroom just cradling the knot pendant in her palm. She didn't want to let go of it completely, not yet. But it was time to put it all to rest. There was no going back to the night Mark was killed and saving him. If that had even been possible. Nothing made that okay, but at least they knew what had happened and the one responsible had officially paid for it.

She let the necklace rain into a silk pouch and locked it away in a compartment of her jewelry case, whispering a good-bye to Mark. It was time to go meet her friends.

Cleaner, breathing easier, and much more at peace, Belinda trotted outside to join Kyle, Jonas, and Bennett, gathered around a crumpled piece of metal that used to be Jonas' bike.

"What happened to it?" Belinda put her hands on her hips.

"I promise I'll pay for a new one," Kyle said to Jonas.

"You ran over his bike?" Belinda said.

"I was in a panic to get to you and I didn't realize it was behind my Jeep."

"I parked it in the grass," Jonas said forlornly. "I thought it would be safe there."

Bennett and Belinda exchanged amused glances. Bennett held an ice pack to the side of his head, looking a little woozy. Belinda frowned. "What will happen to Jarrett?"

"Well, he's guilty of breaking and entering and setting the basement on fire..." Jonas rocked on his feet.

Kyle glanced at him. "You forgot the so-called car accident."

"Byrne actually confessed to driving the car. However, Jarrett has admitted to being an accomplice."

"So is there anything I can do to help him?" Belinda said. She figured Jarrett's future was rocky now, but she also knew the right connections could make a difference.

Kyle looked at her in disbelief. "Help him? Sis, he tried to kill you!"

Cliffhanger

"No, he didn't. He was trying to rescue me. I know he was a little misguided—"

"A little?" Kyle stepped toward her. "Yeah. I'd say he was a little misguided locking you in the basement and rigging the circuit board to light up." Kyle's chest stiffened. "You're the Queen of Misguided Lovers, you know that?"

"Kyle," Belinda said softly, placing a hand on his shoulder. "I don't want this poor kid to end up like Jeff. He needs help."

Jonas glanced from one to the other. "I'm sure we can find a way for you to help out."

"Thank you. I want to do whatever we can to make things right." She patted Kyle's shoulder. If he wanted to go cold on her after everything that had happened, fine. She could go visit with Bennett while he defrosted.

"I know Mr. Trebor's family appreciates Carmichael's legal assistance," Jonas said.

"Pro bono." Bennett looked at Belinda significantly.

"Carmichael's a decent guy." She smiled at Bennett. "For Trebor's sake, though, I just wish he hadn't gone to Lily's."

Jonas sighed. "It's a two-edged sword. On the one hand, he saw you in your bedroom on Lily's computer when he delivered those flowers and recognized that it was some sort of surveillance. If it weren't for that, we wouldn't have known she was using your computer webcam to spy on you. On the other, ignorance is safer—for some of us."

"Not for Stellan."

"No, not for him." Jonas crossed his arms. "He should have called the police and let Jeff tell them that he saw Lily leaving Mark's sailboat the night before. If he had...well, this whole thing would have been over with about ten years ago."

"Are we going to help him too?" Kyle said sarcastically.

Belinda pinched him, but not with much gusto. "He has his own set of lawyers for that. Even with Byrne willingly giving him up, I don't think Stellan will fall too hard for that or over the illegal immigration papers scheme they have going. I foresee him slipping right through the noose and back into his comfy New York City penthouse. But, I do have to say, I actually like him better now than when we were kids."

"And Byrne?" Jonas said. "Will you follow through on your promise to him? Even if he was Lily's right-hand man?"

Belinda had actually forgotten about that. And she knew more about his involvement now than when she'd thrown that out there, but no matter. Her word was her word. "He did cooperate as it turns out, so I guess I don't have a choice. I suppose I can do something so he doesn't take all the blame. Stellan did accept a payout from Lily when he discovered *Sea Stud* in his warehouse, and that was after he told me about Mark. He should have learned his lesson and called the police."

Jonas smirked. "You're quite the woman, Ms. Kittridge."

Belinda gazed over at Bennett. "As my nana always tells me, status is only as good as what you use it for."

Chapter 25

Belinda and Kyle squished up together on the same chair in front of Belinda's laptop. What had been used as an evil spyware tool was now a way to talk to their parents face-to-face across the Atlantic. All four of them waved to each other, talking all at once.

"There's the other one!" Belinda's mom pointed at Kyle. She gripped her chest, her golden brown eyes getting watery. "My twin babies are both okay."

"I'm sorry about the house," Belinda said despondently. She wanted to hug the computer monitor. She hadn't realized how much she needed them through this whole ordeal until they appeared on the screen. "You're going to have to fix the back door too. And the bar glass..."

"We're in Europe," her father interjected, sticking his nose up to the webcam like a curious puppy. "Maybe we'll find a replacement."

"And if not," Rosalind said, "I'll come home to my house in shreds, but not my children."

Her father, Spencer, shrugged. "You have the information. Take care of anything you need."

"Bennett already recommended someone for the circuit board issue," Kyle said. "He's coming tomorrow."

Rosalind squinted into the webcam, flicking back her reddish-brown hair. "Who?"

"Some guy named—"

"Not that!" Rosalind rolled her eyes. "Who's Bennett?"

"He's a friend," Belinda said quickly before Kyle could open his big mouth again.

"Have we met before?"

"Oh, no. He's new. I mean, I only met him when I got back." Belinda could feel her face start to flush.

"Well, that's very nice of him to help out, considering you just met." Rosalind set her knowing eyes on her daughter.

"Bennett helped us out a lot, especially Bels." Kyle leaned across his sister. "The circuit board's kind of a minor thing in comparison." Belinda knew he was trying to help, but she wished he would just stop.

"You'll thank him for us?" Spencer said. "And the police officer who did so much for you?"

Belinda nodded, relieved. Saved by her father's obliviousness.

"So will the two of you survive in the carriage house?" Rosalind said.

Kyle grinned. "She'll keep me in line."

Their parents laughed. "We have no doubt," their father said. "Whatever you do, keep the security system activated from now on. That's why we have one!"

Belinda lit up and opened her mouth, words pouring out before she could really stop herself. "Bennett's coming to help with that later." Rosalind raised her eyebrows and Belinda's face grew warm again. "Kyle did something to the system, and I can't get it to work now. Bennett's in security." Belinda faltered, now gripping her knees. "That's what he does for work."

"He sounds handy."

"Oh, he's very handy," Kyle said in an exaggerated voice. "He was a police officer and did some private investigating, and now he's in event security. His range of expertise has proven invaluable through this whole situation."

Belinda glowered at him.

"Oh, and he loves pancakes. Especially Belinda's."

Kyle would pay for that last remark. Oh, would he pay.

"Kyle ran over your tomato plants with his dirt bike."

"Hey! We had a deal!"

Belinda smiled sweetly. "All bets were off when you said Bennett likes my pancakes."

"Are you done now?" Spencer said, his eyes crinkling around the edges in amusement.

"You destroyed my tomato plants?" Rosalind looked back at her husband with sad eyes.

"Oh, honey. That was never going to work out. I think we established that last year."

Rosalind wrinkled her nose. Belinda and Kyle laughed. There was nothing like a family reunion via video conference, even if they were crazy.

~ * ~

A dance song blared from the carriage house when Bennett drew up in his truck. After knocking several times with no response, he finally just opened the door. Kyle wore a black fedora angled on his head and he and Belinda danced around each other.

Belinda finally saw Bennett and grabbed his hand, dragging him over to their mini dance floor. He stood there while she hopped around and lifted his arm to twirl under it, and she and Kyle shouted the lyrics to the song. Bennett knew they were a lot alike, but this just clarified that their similarities went beyond appearance.

"We earned the title best dance duo by our class," Belinda said proudly.

"You danced together?" Bennett held his ground while Belinda yanked his arms around.

"We went doe and stag to a lot of parties," Kyle said, tilting his fedora so it covered his eyes.

"Doe and stag?"

"Yeah, well, it can't really be just stag if my sister's with me."

Belinda laughed again and held her hands up behind her. "We're celebrating because Kyle just put the last box on top."

Bennett gazed up at the pyramid. It was hardly the most efficient way to organize their stuff, but with little time to move everything and the chaos that had erupted, it was the best Belinda could do. At least the boxes were out of the way so they wouldn't constantly trip over them.

"All Kyle has to do now is haul in our suitcases and we're done," she said, powering down the stereo when the song ended.

"All I have to do?" Kyle huffed. "What's happening to you?"

"I have to go help Bennett." Belinda smiled, twirling over to the door. "And you owe me. Big time."

Kyle opened his mouth to protest but then just nodded agreement.

"Don't forget to sign the card for Nicole. It's on the island."

"What did you and Victoria end up buying?"

"Bar glasses." She smiled. Kyle's face lit up and Belinda led Bennett to the main house. He followed her inside, their footsteps echoing louder without any furniture in the house.

"I think this is the paperwork for the system, but it's just a guess. I forgot to ask Mom and Dad and it's a pain to contact them—the time difference and all." Belinda rolled her eyes at Europe's audacity to be in a different time zone. "But it looks right, don't you think?"

Bennett looked at the crinkled piece of paper and studied the keypad for a minute, already familiar with that type of security system.

"Even Kyle won't be able to argue now, and I don't care if he does. We're using it." Belinda folded her arms over her chest as if that made it a done deal. After hovering around him expectantly, Bennett finally shooed her away. He could reactivate it in seconds, but not with her interrupting him.

Once that was taken care of, Bennett met Belinda on the back porch, bearing two sugar cookies he'd picked up from a bakery en route. Belinda bit into hers, closing her eyes as the cookie melted right on the spot. Bennett enjoyed his with less drama, but he did enjoy the show. "That's a good cookie," Belinda said after she swallowed. Bennett agreed.

"I can resist most sweets, but not sugar cookies."

"So now I know how to bribe you." Belinda's eyes sparkled as she chewed off another piece.

Bennett half-smiled, tilting his head down. "Never give away your tactics."

"Well, I don't think I'd ever actually bribe you, though it might be tempting." She licked sugar off of her fingers. "Though not as tempting as the cookies themselves. I'd probably eat them before I ever got to you."

Bennett munched and they both watched the ripples on the water beyond, the sound of a hammer banging carrying on the wind. Soon enough, Belinda would hear plenty of that racket right there.

"Are you all right with how things turned out?" he said.

Belinda shrugged. "Yes and no. I have a lot of pesky 'what-ifs?'"

"Like what?"

"This may sound far-fetched, but I started to wonder if Jeff's issues were just tied up with what he knew about Mark. Maybe he just needed someone to talk to."

Bennett frowned. "I don't think I would say it's far-fetched, but pointless to speculate now. If he did hope to tell you, he could have taken a much better approach. Or, better yet, spoken to someone who could have actually helped him."

"I could've helped."

"Let me rephrase then. He should have spoken with someone older. You were too young to become his confidant about a potential murder case."

Belinda had to agree with him there. "I still feel terrible about it. Worse knowing that Lily tried to put the blame on Kyle for the whole thing."

"Kyle, Stellan. Whoever was convenient I think."

"One positive development has come from all of this though."

Indeed, Bennett thought. "What's that?"

"Kyle is refurbishing Mark's old sailboat and getting back to sailing himself this summer." Belinda beamed. "It's been so long and I was beginning to give up hope that he would ever sail again."

"Ever is a long time."

"True. But he did have legitimate reasons to stay away."

"I guess he now has legitimate reasons to return to it."

Belinda glanced at him shyly. "Maybe you can come out with us sometime. If you have room in your schedule. I know you're busy."

"I'll make room." Bennett smiled. That true smile that she'd seen once while they fished on the rocks and his eyes turned velvety gray.

Belinda's face did that glowing thing it did a lot when she was pleased, her heart fluttering at the thought that Bennett Tate would make room for her, and she took another bite of her cookie. If he kept bringing her sweets, he might have to make room for her in more ways than one.

About the Author

Amy Saunders is a mystery lover with a soft spot for humor and romance—and the ocean. So it's appropriate that her first series encompasses all of these elements. She's also the author of three standalone mysteries and one short story. Learn more about Amy and her books at amyandthepen.wordpress.com.

Coming Soon...

Auf'd (The Belinda & Bennett Mysteries, Book 2)!

If you enjoyed *Cliffhanger*, please leave a review at Amazon, Goodreads, etc.!

Visit amyandthepen.wordpress.com and join my email newsletter to learn about future releases.

Printed in Poland
by Amazon Fulfillment
Poland Sp. z o.o., Wrocław